MAFIA'S DIRTY SECRET

MAFIA'S OBSESSION BOOK 1

SUMMER COOPER

D1715991

ALSO BY SUMMER COOPER

Read Summer's sexiest and most popular
romance books.

DARK DESIRES SERIES
Dark Desire
Dark Rules
Dark Secret
Dark Time
Dark Truth

An Amazon Top 100
A sexy romantic comedy
Somebody To Love

An Amazon Top 100
A 5-book billionaire romance box set
Filthy Rich
Summer's other box sets include:
Too Much To Love
Down Right Dirty

Mafia's Obsession
A hot mafia romance series
Mafia's Dirty Secret
Mafia's Fake Bride
Mafia's Final Play

Screaming Demons
An MC romance series full of suspense
Take Over
Rough Start
Rough Ride
Rough Choice
New Era
Rough Patch
Rough Return
Rough Road
New Territory

Rough Trip
Rough Night
Rough Love

Check out Summer's entire collection at
www.summercooper.com/books

Happy reading,
Summer Cooper
xoxo

ACKNOWLEDGMENTS

I'd like to give special thanks to

Savvy
who's helped me get the books out to the
world.

Terri and Tasha
for being the best and most supportive
editing team.

Jenny
for designing this book cover.

My family
for being supportive and believing in my
dreams.

Last but not least
My ARC Team
My Readers
My Publisher

Lot of love,
Summer
xoxo

Marie ran the warm washcloth down her mother's rigid arm. The tremors were worse today, she noted as she washed the soap from her mother's skin. The washcloth moved down to the tips of the woman's fingers, and Marie noted for the millionth time that her mother still had slim, shapely fingers.

She dipped the cloth in the pink, plastic basin that had come from... somewhere. The hospital on her mother's last visit, that was where they got it, she remembered now. She brushed black, silky strands of her hair from her naturally tan face with the back of her hand and looked away from her mother. It was too hot to work like this, but she couldn't afford anyone else to help her.

A tear slid down her face, but she swiped it away angrily. Self-pity wasn't something she'd often allowed herself to wallow in, but sometimes it was hard not to. Her mother had lost all ability to care for herself, and it was now down to Marie to do it for her.

"Mar-..." came her mother's garbled voice. Sometimes the woman could barely speak, and at others, her voice was clearer. Marie brushed short, white hair from her mother's face. A face that had once been on movie posters, with shiny dark-brown hair and sassy eyes was now little more than a shell of what used to be. All that French and Spanish heritage had melted with time, into the face of a woman old before her time.

"I know, Mom, I'm trying to hurry." Marie moved to the other side of her mother's hospital bed, made sure the blue plastic pads with an absorbent center protected the sheets, and began to wash her mother's other side. Then she'd work on the middle, her back, and finally, her legs and feet.

It was a process she'd learned from the home health agency that paid her wages. As her mother's own Personal Care Assistant, she was paid to do the tasks Ruby wouldn't have allowed someone else to do. It allowed Marie to have an income, take care of her mother, and kept them both fed. A state agency paid for it all, some program or another that Marie had signed her mother up for a long time ago. That was back when she first had to use a wheelchair and could get out of bed.

Back when Marie had been on her way to Louisiana State University with dreams in her head and hope in her heart. Now, she was her mother's slave, the same as always. At least now she didn't have to be verbally abused too. Her mother could barely speak, even when she was lucid, and that kept her sharp tongue in check.

Marie felt terrible for the thought and winced as she promised she'd do penance later. For now, she had to wash her mother's torso, then the rest. She always tried to think of something else as she went through the task she'd been trained to do. She'd think of the beach she wanted to go to, or the restaurants not far away. She'd think about what she'd order from the menu, and what she would do once she had her toes in the sand.

Marie left the small room with blacked-out windows. They'd done that to protect her mother's eyes. She'd claimed the light hurt, but Marie had often wondered if it was to keep the world at bay. If she couldn't see out, nobody could see in. It had always been that way. All of her life, Ruby hid them both from the world, from outsiders as she'd called them.

Once she was done with her mother's torso, the young woman walked into the bathroom just opposite the bedroom her mother had claimed and rinsed out the tub.

As she filled it with warm, clean water, Marie hummed to herself, a song she'd heard on the radio. Cajun music was her favorite, and she often left the radio playing, even when she went to sleep.

"Unwan...," Ruby groaned as Marie came in.

Marie sighed, but let it go. "Unwanted bitch", that's what her mother was trying to say. Even now, when Marie did all she could to keep her clean, free from bedsores, and in clean clothes, her mother was cruel.

She always had been though.

Marie had always known that she wasn't wanted. She could remember her mother saying it when she was two years old, then three, then every year after. Even when Marie was 18 and ready to leave her mother, at long last, her mother had said it. She'd spit it that day, but she'd added a new twist.

Ungrateful.

Marie was ungrateful for the long, miserable life her mother gave her. That's how she'd announced the news that she was sick, she'd called Marie an ungrateful, unwanted bitch that wouldn't even stick around to take care of her sick mother. Marie had only wanted to escape the torment, but she'd cracked and stayed.

Her mother's Parkinson's had progressed enough that the doctors had finally stopped blaming the car accident that had killed Marie's father and nearly took her mother's life. They'd done round after round of tests and finally concluded that the tremors, the loss of balance, and the rigidity in her mother's left arm was from Parkinson's disease. It was at an advanced stage by then, and Marie was as doomed as her mother.

Doomed to always be there for her.

Marie felt guilt over her quiet anger, her resentment of her mother. She knew she should have been a better daughter, that she should try harder for her mother, but some days, like today, the resentment got the better of her. It was hot, sticky hot, and flies were buzzing around already. The mosquitos would come later, breaking through the mosquito nets to leave her with itchy welts.

She wanted out of this place, to be somewhere where she could afford air conditioning, where someone else took care of her mother. Where she wasn't a slave to a woman that had hated her for her very existence.

"You were supposed to be aborted, that's what your father wanted. But we had the accident, and here you are, all mouth and selfish." She could remember her mother saying that to her when she was five and needed new shoes because she'd outgrown the old ones.

Marie had learned to just make do with what she had until her mother noticed her clothes didn't fit, or the school called her to threaten they'd report her if she didn't take better care of her little girl. Those days had been the worst because Marie would come home to a raging, hateful mother that pulled at her arms until it left bruises as she dragged her daughter out to the car, into a store, and threw her down to try on clothes or shoes. Or bras.

She shuddered as she remembered the first time her mother took her to shop for bras. There'd been hisses about how her daughter wouldn't turn out to be a little slut and no she couldn't have the soft, lacy bras that were comfortable; she'd wear this plain cotton contraption that was so tight it left lines around her ribcage.

Her mother wasn't the sweet and loving angel so many other kids around her had. Not at all.

Marie scrubbed at her mother's back, checked her skin while she dried it for signs that she might be getting bedsores, and moisturized the skin. She picked up another washcloth, a clean one, and then she tackled her mother's privates, a job she hated to do. It felt like she was doing something wrong. She knew it needed to be done, that her mother had to be clean everywhere, but damn if it didn't feel like an invasion.

She hummed another song as she slid the cloth down around the necessary parts, her brain frozen, no thoughts entered at all, as she pulled the cloth out, rinsed it, then rinsed the soap away. More clean water. She'd have to do the laundry today, get it hung out on a line, and then brought back in. When she got back from the grocery store, she'd take it all down and fold it up.

She was nearly done now, only her legs and feet. Marie inspected her mother's heels, the back of her calves and thighs, any pressure points, and decided to put on the special boots the doctor gave her to protect her mother's feet. They kept the heels off the bed, and suspended so there would be no pressure, and thus, no sores.

She checked her mother's elbows one more time, and finally took the tub away. She cleaned the blue tub with hot water and put it on a rack to dry. She'd need it again in the evening. Or if her mother had an accident. It happened sometimes, and Marie would have to wash her up again if it did.

Her mother wasn't gone, mentally, it was just physical, her mother's problem. Sometimes she would hallucinate or show signs of dementia, but it wasn't often. Not yet, anyway. Marie knew what the future held as her mother's disease progressed and was ready for it. She hoped.

She went into the kitchen and sat down at the table to rest. It was topped with cheap plastic, with wood particles coming free from the edges. It was probably older than Ruby herself, but it was all they could afford now. Once the house hadn't looked so bad, Marie knew. Her mother had made a little money from the film she made, and every now and then, she'd still get a royalty check. Not often, but every now and then.

It had been enough, back then, to buy the five-bedroom house with two bathrooms, and two floors. Most of the rooms were empty now, and the doors stayed closed. In the winter it was too hard to warm rooms that were never used anyway. She'd sold the items inside the rooms, to pay for her mother's care, and to pay the bills. Now, her mother had a disability check, and government medical insurance, but it didn't pay for everything.

At least Marie was getting paid to take care of her. If she'd had to do it without pay, she might have lost her mind as she struggled to pay bills. Or starved, because there was no way she could do both. Another state program paid for a nurse to come once a day, and check Ruby's vitals and her overall health. The nurse would stay for an hour, and that was the only real break Marie had from her home.

That was when she'd run her errands, get the shopping done, and escape. Sometimes, she'd go to the library, pick up some books, something she'd read at night, in bed, to help her get to sleep. Some days, she couldn't relax enough to fall asleep, and reading would always help her out.

"Mar-...," The loud sound interrupted

her moment of peace, and Marie stood up. She smoothed her hand down her still damp jeans and took a deep breath. She knew what that sound meant. A mess had been made.

She picked up a box of gloves, the paper towels she kept off to the side for these occasions and picked up some plastic bags from the grocery store. The smell hit her as she walked down the hallway, a smell that confirmed her suspicions. She'd have to clean her mother up, wash her again, and maybe even change the bed.

She'd put fresh absorbent pads underneath her mother when she'd finished washing her, but they weren't always enough. She made one stop, in the bathroom she found a jar of mentholated ointment and swiped a couple of globs up her nose, then went into her mother's bedroom. The sadistic leer on her mother's face told her this was no accident.

Sometimes her mother was just a cruel, heartless bitch, Marie had to admit. She tried so hard to be a good girl, she thought, she tried to not be mean, to not give in to her mother's nastiness but sometimes, she hated herself for it but, sometimes she really looked forward to the day this was all over.

Marie pursed her lips and ignored the garbled cackle her mother made as she pulled the sheet down from Ruby's legs. Even the mentholated ointment couldn't keep that out of her nose, but she reminded herself not to breathe through her nose and got on with the task at hand. An hour later, just as she heard a knock at the back door, Marie was done. She'd cleaned up the worst of it, washed her mother, changed the sheets and her mother's nightdress, and had put fresh pads down.

She walked out of the room, determined not to cry. She wanted to, she wanted to so much, but she wouldn't. She remembered the way her mother had tried to use her good arm, her right arm, to push Marie's face down into the mess she'd made and felt her eyes well up. How could being born deserve so much cruelty?

She knew her mother said her father wanted her aborted, but the hateful woman never said what she'd wanted before the accident. She'd only ever said it was too late once she'd woken up and the whole world knew about her pregnancy. That no doctor would do it at that advanced state anyway. Marie suspected her mother had wanted to keep her but had changed her mind once her father died.

Marie was a bright woman, had always done well in school, and had made good grades. She was able to deduce, from what her mother had said over the years, sometimes after a few glasses of cheap wine, that her mother had become pregnant on purpose, to trap the man she'd wanted to force to marry her.

But he'd already been married to another woman, and then he'd died. Her plan, her trap, had failed.

It wasn't the kind of past people would

be proud of, for her or her mother, and her mother drank a lot when Marie was a child. She'd probably said things she didn't remember saying. Marie didn't mention those things or ask about them, for fear of her mother's anger. She'd been slapped one too many times to push her luck.

She was 26 now, and she'd spent 8 years in this miserable hell. At first, it hadn't been so bad. She'd been able to take her mother out with her, or she'd been able to go out on her own. Within a year, however, Ruby had taken to her bed and had refused to leave it. Of course, her left leg and arm wouldn't move, and the effects on her spine and hips made movement difficult, so Marie couldn't really blame her, but she'd wondered how much of her mother's problems were exaggerated.

In quiet moments, like now when she was headed into town for groceries in the old battered car that barely ran but tried, more thoughts would intrude. Her mother had always been cruel. She could be making this worse for Marie than it had to be. It was within the realm of possibility anyway.

At those times, Marie would think that maybe she could be a better daughter. But Ruby could have, also, been a much better mother.

2

Marie turned into the slight bend in the road with practiced ease. She'd driven the road so many times, she could have made each movement simply from the sound of the tires on the road. A deep sound meant she was on the road just outside of her house, a softer sound, like cloth swishing over metal, meant she was on the bend that came just after the house, the part that led into town and the stores.

Then there were the shadows. She knew where each tall Cypress tree stood, each one dripping with Spanish moss, or where each Tupelo tree stood, and where each shadow was supposed to be now. She'd traveled this road practically every day of her life. Each shadow gave her a point of reference as she drove along.

The law said you had to drive with your eyes open though, Marie thought with a shadow of a smile, so she kept them open. She saw the same old 'for sale' sign on a trailer off to the right as she made a stop at the crossing that would take her into town. The tobacco shop had new prices up today, though, the bright orange letters were hard to miss. Mr. Theriot still had his crawfish traps for sale on his front lawn, across the street from the small car dealership that always managed to get new stock but never seemed to sell any cars.

The town of Mary's Point, always a quiet place, but so full of life. At least, to Marie, it seemed so. Her ancestors had lived here over 200 years ago, they'd made their lives here, and now Marie and her mother Ruby were the last of her family.

There were others, spread out all over the state, and the country, but only Marie and Ruby had stayed put. Well, Ruby left for a while, and Marie had tried to escape the place but hadn't quite accomplished it.

She drove past the small library, the two small banks that were always in competition, over the small drawbridge over the bayou, and pulled to a stop to turn in at the grocery store. On her right was a gas station/fast food restaurant, and to her left was the store. A little further down the road were more houses, an apartment building, and a few other offices and boutiques. There was even a café that sold café au lait and beignets, but Marie didn't get to go there too often.

She wouldn't get to do today either, she had to pick up groceries, her mother's medicine, see Ruby's doctor about a form the government insurance wanted him to fill out, and then get home before the nurse's hour was up. It was a real blessing to have the woman come for an hour every day, but sometimes it just wasn't long enough. Marie knew she had to make do, though, it was all she'd ever done.

She could smell the water of the bayou as she stepped out of the old car she'd inherited from her mother. The old Ford had been bought new, but that was back when Marie was still a baby. It had been cared for, though, and still ran. Most of the time. She carefully shut the door, locked it, and went into the cool air of the store. It was always a relief, that first moment when she walked into the brightly lit building.

The store was locally owned and stocked furniture, clothing, groceries, and just about anything else anybody would need, stuck out here in the sticks. Marie took a shopping cart and began to walk through the store. She saw a new display over in the furniture section, new sofas, and decorations for a bedroom. She saw a white and black comforter on a new bed display too, that she really liked. Black filigree on a white background, so Louisiana, but so out of her budget, too.

Marie looked away without even so much as a sigh. She'd learned long ago, things like that just weren't for her. She sped along into the grocery department and began to fill the basket with the small amounts of food she'd need for the week. Her mother sometimes had trouble swallowing now so Marie had learned to make soft foods for her. Being in bed all the time meant her mother didn't require a lot of food anyway, but the dietitian that came showed her what to feed her mother and how much. If her mother asked, she'd give her more, but usually getting her to eat one meal could be a huge challenge.

She made quick work of the task and was soon outside again in the damp heat. Her green t-shirt stuck to her and her thighs began to stick together below the legs of her shorts. At least she had on flip flops today. Socks and shoes would have been all but unbearable in a car with no air conditioning.

A slight boom in the air and the sound of a very powerful engine drew her attention as she put the groceries in the trunk of the old white car. What should have been a glance up, turned into a look of shock at what she saw. A black Lamborghini, probably from some time in the 1960s, was parked at the gas station. The car was unlike anything she'd ever seen before and screamed expensive luxury. That wasn't what shocked her though.

It was the handsome, well-built man with a mop of black hair that pumped gas into the car that shocked her. He glanced around vacantly as if nothing about the surrounding area mattered to him and he couldn't be more bored. That look didn't take away from the beauty of his face though. Even from this distance, Marie could tell the man would stop heartbeats all over the world.

He had the smoldering looks of the

Italian models she'd seen in magazines in the pharmacy as she waited to be served. Usually, ads for underwear or cologne that she'd always speed past. His nose wasn't too big, or too curved, it was just right on a face with high cheekbones, full lips, and a jaw-line that looked as if an artist had sculpted it.

The expensive clothes he wore showed off an equally sculpted body, and she wondered how many hours he spent in a gym to get that built. He glanced in her direction as if he felt her stare, and Marie quickly looked away. She tucked a lock of hair behind her ear and pushed her cheap sunglasses down on her face. Hopefully, he hadn't seen her gawping at him.

She pushed the cart back to the stand, in a daze as she berated herself for her childishness. She'd never had a boyfriend, her mother hadn't allowed it, and she'd never really been accepted at school. As the illegitimate child of a failed starlet, she was an outcast even before she'd started school. In this rural part of Louisiana, Catholicism reigned and her mother had sinned. Sinned so much she'd been excommunicated.

Marie's cheeks flamed as she remembered it all over again, how her mother had screamed profanities in the middle of mass, drunk and angry because her latest lover had gone back to his wife. The church spent years trying to aid her mother, in trying to get her to change her ways, but when she'd screamed there was no God, and that she'd do those awful things to the holy family, well, she'd left the church little choice. That was all before Marie had even started school. It only got worse after that.

Ruby had time to go the bar before Marie came home from school, once she'd shipped her daughter off to the local elementary school. Sometimes, those trips out for a few hours became days. Ruby would leave Marie to fend for herself while she spent her evenings at the dance halls, trying to find a man that would help her forget her woes. Marie had learned early on to watch what she said, how she dressed, and how often she bathed.

Somebody had called social services on Ruby when Marie was in the first grade. After Ruby had played the perfect mother to get the social worker off her back, Marie had been beaten with a belt until she was black and blue. She'd also gone three days without food. That part hadn't bothered her as much as the bruises hidden beneath her clothes.

She was used to her mother not bringing home food or taking her out to eat. Hunger was familiar, the pain wasn't something she could forget, though. It had all come together to create a quiet child, one that observed, but rarely spoke. Now an adult, Marie wasn't much different to the child that had always been on the lookout for trouble that might come her mother's way.

The drinking had hidden Ruby's condition for a long time, but eventually, it had caught up with her. Marie was almost glad about the disease slowly taking her mother away from her. At least her mother didn't come home battered and used up now. Which was another disloyal thought, Marie reminded herself.

She wasn't overly religious, she couldn't be with her mother there to disillusion her, but she was a firm believer in karma and all that entailed. She knew she'd pay for every disloyal, unkind thought she had about her mother, in one way or another. Her mother couldn't help it, after all, she'd had a really hard life since she'd had Marie.

That's the line Ruby drilled into her, over the years, every time she did something that made her life a little bit harder. Marie had to sacrifice her own happiness because Ruby deserved the little pleasures she gained from the life of her own making. Marie took a deep breath, realized she'd been standing at the cart stand way too long, and quickly turned around.

The sound of brakes and a powerful engine finally broke into her reverie as she saw a big black sports car had almost run her over. Marie gaped at the windshield, her hands on the hood of the car. Slowly, thoughts began to trickle in…

…the man from the gas station. He was so… beautiful. Gorgeous. And he was out of the car, in front of her now.

She stared up, way up, at the most intriguing eyes she'd ever seen. He'd pushed his sunglasses up over his head, and he looked down at her now with concern. She smiled, lost in his eyes for a moment.

"Are you alright?" a deeply accented voice asked. Not from around here then. "Miss?"

"Pardon?" Her eyebrows crooked over her eyes in question as she shifted on her feet and looked up at him.

"I nearly hit you, are you alright?" His lips, so full and sensual she wanted to touch them with her fingertips, just to feel their softness, caught her eyes, and again, she forgot to answer him.

"Miss?"

"What?" Suddenly, she snapped out of her daze, her cheeks flamed into twin red flags, and she dropped her head down to look at her feet. "Sorry, yes, I'm fine."

She waved at her car and looked up at him, the left side of her face scrunched up with embarrassment. He smiled, nodded, and looked down at her with interest now that she wasn't a zombie.

"Good. You scared me, I didn't even see you there at the stand, until you turned around. My fault, entirely."

"No, it was mine. I wasn't paying any attention. Sorry, I'll let you be on your way now." She smiled and turned away, but something made her look back. He hadn't moved a muscle, he just watched her as she walked away with something that could be? No, it couldn't be interest. Men didn't look at her like that.

He drove away as she got into her car, and she thought about how nice it had been to speak with him. Most people avoided any possibility of talking with her if they could. It was almost as if they thought she'd blight them if she spoke to them. She'd learned to do most transactions quietly, and was used to only having conversations with her mother's doctor, nurse, and the pharmacist.

She'd sometimes have to speak to others, to take care of business matters for her mother, but not very often, and those people didn't live here. It was nice to actually talk to someone. She drove away, headed back to the house, hidden almost in the swamp, that her mother bought all those years ago. It was much too large for them, with way too many bedrooms on two floors.

They didn't need all that and there hadn't been a soul upstairs in months now. Marie went up every now and then to check the ceilings and check for damage after a storm, but otherwise, there was no need to go up there. She kept up the two bedrooms they slept in, the living room, kitchen, bathroom, and the laundry room. That was enough.

Her mother was asleep when she arrived home, so Marie put the groceries away after the nurse left. She put on some pasta to cook on the stove, a little bit of spaghetti sauce she'd put in the freezer went into the microwave, and her radio came on.

With her feet propped on another chair, Marie allowed the sound of swamp pop music to take her away to a land where a man like the Lamborghini driver noticed her. He'd take her to dance the night away at the dance hall, or out to eat at some fancy restaurant tucked away in a secret part of New Orleans. He'd sweep her off her feet and take her away from this miserable life, with the flash of a pearly white grin and a blink of those warm brown eyes. Life would be good, something she'd never known before, and she wouldn't have to hear her mother's voice telling her she was unwanted, ever again.

"Marie!" Came the strangled sound of

her mother's voice, ruined by the cigarettes she used to smoke and the paralyzed muscles caused by her condition. "Marie, I'm wet!"

That, Marie thought with a sigh filled with regret. That's what she wanted to escape, just for a few short hours, even if it meant she'd go to hell for the thought. That voice, that hateful, anger-strained voice. She turned off the stove and pulled a pair of gloves from the boxes she had strewn around the house. She'd never escape, her mother wouldn't allow it.

3

A beam of sunlight danced across the pages of Marie's book as the wind rustled gently through the leaves in the tree. It reminded her that she didn't have all day to sit there at the café with her book. She finished her beignets and took the last sip of her café au lait before she put the book in her bag, gathered her things, and got up to leave.

A dress in the little boutique next door caught her eye and she wandered over. It was a party dress, as her mother would call it. Short, designed to be tight, in a vivid red that would suit her coloring perfectly. The kind of dress she'd never get to wear.

She looked at the other dresses in the shop window and couldn't help but smile. There was a dress that glittered, one that was far too risqué in black leather, and another that would be suitable for an outdoor event with a feminine floral pattern in bold blues and reds. The kind of dresses that women with manicures and hairstyles that didn't come from a pair of paper cutting scissors and the air would wear.

Marie glanced down at her hands and winced. They were red and raw from all the washing she did. Hygiene was key to keeping her mother healthy, and that meant she washed her hands, a lot. She used hand moisturizer on them, but nothing ever seemed to take away the angry red that appeared around her knuckles and the fingertips. Her nails were clean and white on the tips, but they were short, a necessity when taking care of a bedridden patient.

She could look at those dresses all she

wanted to but she knew she'd never have a reason to wear one. There were no parties to attend and she couldn't afford one of those dresses, even if she did have somewhere to wear it to. It was nice to look though. Especially since she still had the man from a few days ago on her mind.

These were the kinds of dresses a woman he'd date would wear. That one in leather, with a pair of black stiletto heels, would be just his style, for his woman to wear that is. He'd probably pick a blond or a redhead with pouty lips and bedroom eyes. A glance in the window told her that her brown eyes were alright, but there were dark circles under them. Her mother had kept her up most of the night with a screaming fit that wouldn't end. She'd finally given her a sedative the doctor prescribed for these episodes, and she'd been able to get to bed. So what if the sun had just started to rise, she'd needed those two hours before she had to get up and greet the world again.

Marie's fingers fluttered at the ends of her hair and noted how jagged the edges were before they dropped down. She had on another pair of faded out denim shorts, with a black t-shirt and her usual cheap black flip flops. A man like that wouldn't notice her. Except… he had. Kind of. Okay, it was only because he'd almost run her over, but still, he'd noticed.

That smile came back, the one that she'd discovered on her face not long after the incident at the grocery store. She'd see it in flashes as she passed a mirror or the black darkness of a television screen that hadn't been turned on. He'd given her a reason to smile, even if he didn't know it.

The guy was probably long gone, though. The town was the kind of place tourists came to in the summer, or during the various hunting seasons. People that wanted to save a few dollars by stopping at a hotel just outside of New Orleans would come here, drive into the city, and then come back at night. The hunters always went out into the swamps, and might not be seen for days. She'd never seen a car like that around here, though. He wasn't on a budget vacation, and he certainly wasn't a hunter.

A traveler lost and in search of directions, maybe? But surely a man with a car like that would have GPS? It was hard to say, she decided and turned away from the glass. As soon as she faced the road a car went by. A black car with curves and lines that were now familiar. Somehow, she wasn't the least bit surprised to see the car, and the man, drive past just then. She should have been, she knew that, but she wasn't. There was something special about him, something different, and she had a feeling, a very odd feeling as she watched the car disappear down the road, that she'd meet him again.

Marie knew it wasn't just that he was rich that caught her eye, there had been rich men here before, or the fact that he was handsome. There were plenty of hard-bodied, eye-catching men in the town, so it wasn't that either. She'd felt something when she saw him at the gas station. Something tight and exciting in her chest, that made her want to… dance.

But, he hadn't seen her, she thought as his car disappeared into the distance. Most people didn't, and normally, that was okay. There was something about him, though, that made her want to be noticed. Usually, she liked being in the shadows, always on the edge of the peripheral vision of those around her. It was quiet there, and peaceful.

Yet, something in her wanted him to see her again, to notice her, to take her away to a new and exciting place where "unwanted" was never groaned out at her. Maybe that was it, she wondered as she got back into her car and turned on the radio. Maybe she wanted to be noticed, really noticed, for a change.

Her fingers tapped on the steering wheel, in time with the song that drifted out of the car's speakers. It was a Cajun song, sung in the Cajun French that her mother wouldn't allow her to learn. She'd caught on to bits and pieces over the years, it was impossible not to, but her mother didn't want her to learn it. Early in her life, her mother told her it was the language of the past and that people needed to let it go. Even if it was their heritage.

"Americans speak English, Marie, and so will you. I won't have some backward, backwoods, language coming out of your mouth." Marie could remember her mother saying that so long ago, more than once.

She'd never understood why her mother thought it was backward, it was beautiful, the patois of generations of people combined into a musical sound that she wanted to know. In the end, it didn't matter if she could understand the language the song was sung in. The notes of emotion in the singer's voice told her all she needed to know.

A short time later, she drove through the crumbling brick entrance to the driveway to the house. Jasmine lined both sides of the entrance. Marie noted all of them needed to be pruned, but she rarely had time to do it. Maybe she could get the boy that mowed the lawn to do it, for a little extra than his normal pay. She'd ask him when he came by later in the week.

She pulled up to the house, parked the car, and took out the bags she'd collected. One from the pharmacy, one from the grocery store, and one from the library. She'd picked out a few books to read, and had started one while she was at the café earlier. Hopefully, her mother would be asleep when she got in so she could continue to read.

"Is that you, Marie? You lazy trollop, you've left me for hours in here alone. What kind of ungrateful bitch does that?"

Marie's shoulders sagged and the weight of the bags in her arms pulled them even lower. Not only was her mother awake, but she'd also regained her speech. It happened sometimes, the ability to speak would come and go. It made Marie wonder sometimes if perhaps her mother was acting. She'd been on the verge of being a star when she was in that accident, maybe Ruby had found a way to get even more attention.

Marie would remind herself at those times that the doctor had confirmed the disease, and that Ruby had always been contrary. She'd fight the disease, just to spite Marie and keep her around. She wouldn't give up, or fake being more ill than she was.

"It's me, Mom. I'll be in there in a minute." She put the bags on the table as the nurse walked in.

"She's not herself today," the nurse spoke softly, her eyes sympathetic.

Marie was ashamed of the way her mother spoke to her and of the things she'd said. She couldn't look the older woman in the eye.

"It's hard on her, Jane." Marie glanced over the middle-aged woman with gray hair and soft brown eyes. "Besides, she's not in her right mind. You know I've only been gone an hour. She knows that too, somewhere in her muddled brain."

"I don't know how you do it, Marie, but you're a saint for doing it. I'll see you tomorrow, honey. Take care of yourself." She patted Marie's cheek and Marie felt the prickle of tears in her eyes.

The fact that someone understood what she went through every day made her feel emotional. Or perhaps it was that slight touch, a sign of affection the woman sometimes gave her. Jane had visited almost every day for the last two years and had become a part of Marie and Ruby's lives. That occasional dose of affection always made her eyes well up.

"Bye, Jane. See you tomorrow." Marie watched her leave, made sure the screen door on the back entrance closed all the way, then went to the box of gloves. She put on a pair of the purple gloves and headed in to check on her mother.

Ruby's face, lined deeply now with age

and the stress of her disease, stared up at Marie with disgust. Marie ignored it and pulled her mother's thin blanket to check the absorbent pads beneath her. She'd learned over the years how to tell damp pads from dry through the gloves and found them dry now.

She saw the nurse had put the boots on her, designed for bedridden patients that couldn't move around a lot. They were meant to keep her heels from getting bed-sores. Her mother hated them, but they were necessary. It was something her mother's general practitioner had stressed to her over and over again. Make sure the patient doesn't get bed sores because they were dangerous.

Marie ignored the protests of her mother and checked her skin, from head to toe, to make sure there were no blisters or redness. Those were the first signs that the skin was breaking down and needed to be cared for. Marie didn't find anything and positioned her mother on her side. With the help of a few well-placed pillows, Ruby wouldn't be able to turn on her back. She would spend every hour of the day on her back if she was allowed. That wasn't good for her skin. Marie would let her go on her back in an hour, and then she'd turn her to the other side for a while.

This was one of the reasons Marie didn't sleep well. Her mother had to be moved around constantly, even during the hours when Marie wanted to sleep. It meant her sleep cycle was interrupted often, and sometimes it was hard to get back to sleep. On good days, her mother was able to turn herself and Marie was able to sleep through the night. That didn't happen as often as Marie needed it to.

"You hate me," Ruby rattled out, her eyes dulled by her disease and the medicine she was on. "You've always hated me since the day you were born."

It was a common complaint, and Marie didn't respond. Her mother never seemed to realize that it was hard to hold affection

44

for someone that told you that you were unwanted and unloved. Maybe Ruby's disease caused these moments where she'd forget the past. It used to be the fact that Ruby drank too much, she'd often forget what she did or said after a binge. Now, it was the disease, Marie was certain.

Marie moved to the end of the bed, threw her used gloves in the trash, and picked up the bedding she'd left to be washed when she came home. "I'll be in the laundry room for a little while, Mom. What do you want me to put on the television?"

"You'll let me die here, alone. I know you will, you ungrateful bitch," Ruby said to the wall

Marie rolled her eyes, pursed her lips, and stared at her mother's figure in the bed. "Mom, what do you want to watch?"

"Piss off."

Another roll of her eyes was accompanied by a deep sigh before Marie picked up the remote control and turned the television on. A program that Ruby normally liked was already on the channel so she left it and took the bedding out of the bedroom.

She walked into a room that had been added on sometime in the 1950s. It was decorated all in white and brightly lit from the windows at the end of the room. They spanned across the wall, halfway up. It was one of Marie's favorite rooms, and she spent a lot of time there, especially in the winter. The dryer made the room especially warm then, and she'd spend as much time as she could in there. During the summer, it would become way too hot, but opening the windows usually helped a little.

Marie put the bedclothes in the washer, filled the dispensers, and sat down at the long table pushed up against one wall. The length of the table made folding laundry much easier but for now, it was a nice spot to sit and read.

Only, Marie couldn't concentrate on the book just then. Her brain was too busy wondering about the man in the black car. Would his house have a laundry room?

With the same kind of long table? A table strong enough to hold two, she wondered with a naughty smirk. The fantasy played out as the washer stopped filling with water and began to rotate. The smile didn't leave her face.

4

"Thank you so much for staying a little longer, Jane. I don't know how long it will take, but hopefully not long. You know how it can be with these things," Marie said as she rushed around the kitchen, her head already on the frustrating lines that were always present at the motor vehicle registration place.

"I do, honey. Take your time. The patient I see after your mother is in the hospital, so I'm free for an extra hour or so." Jane pulled at the hem of her pink uniform top and gave a shake of her head. "I'll be here."

"Thanks," Marie said warmly and finally left the house.

She thought about what she needed to do as she drove to the parish seat, to get to the courthouse. The motor vehicle office was there, and she'd probably be there a while. There were always long lines when she went, and she didn't have time to waste.

She groaned in frustration when she was caught by a train, and then trapped behind a huge cart headed for one of the sugarcane farms. The yellow cart drove along slowly, and every time Marie tried to pass the cart, there was oncoming traffic.

By the time she arrived at the courthouse and parked, her nerves were strung tight, and she was in an even bigger rush than she had been. She was going through her bag, looking for her wallet, when she bumped into someone. She apologized automatically and then gaped when she saw who it was.

"It's you," she whispered with surprise.

She felt the corners of her lips twitch up and her cheeks started to burn. With a shake of her head, she continued. "I'm so sorry. It's me that did the bumping this time. I'm really sorry. I was in such a rush to get to the registration office, well. I'm sorry."

Her voice trailed off as she looked up at him, and noted he looked a little older than she'd thought he was. Not much older than her but he had her by a few years if the very faint lines around his eyes were any indication. Or maybe he'd spent more time outdoors than she had and his features were weathered?

"Don't apologize, it's nothing. I wasn't paying attention either." His smile revealed straight, gleaming white teeth. His teeth were perfect except for his right incisor, which had been chipped at some point, but obviously never repaired. Marie wondered why but didn't dare ask.

Her head dropped down, and she pushed a lock of hair behind her right ear.

"I guess you need to be on your way. Sorry about this, again."

"I do, but it was nice to bump into you again." He didn't look to be in a hurry now, and for a moment, Marie forgot that she was too.

"I, well, it's nice to see you again." She noted the look of interest he gave her and was glad she'd put on a nice light-blue blouse and a white skirt that flowed down to her knees for this outing. She looked decent at least.

"Men only want one thing out of us females, Marie and you'd best believe me. They're all pigs, after what's in your pants so they can get their rocks off and then dump you like a piece of used up trash when they're done." Ruby's drunken rant from all those years ago came back to haunt her as the man looked her up and down. His eyebrows lifted in appreciation, even as her mother's voice carried on in her head.

"Don't be a slut, Marie, I won't abide a slut in my home. You go to school, you learn, then

you come home. That's the law, I have to send you. Otherwise, I'd keep you here, away from those boys that can ruin your life if you let them."

Only, Ruby wasn't here now, she didn't feel the way Marie's heartbeat skipped for an instant, or the way her lungs went tight as she looked directly into those dark brown eyes. They were amazing eyes that sucked her in until she actually began to lean towards him.

"I guess I'll see you again, sometime," he said after a long pause. "Take care."

The shrill sound of his phone broke the silence in the long hallway and the inter-lude. Marie nodded, stupidly she thought, and walked away. She'd lost more time, but she didn't mind, not when it meant she'd bumped into *him* again. The line wasn't as long as she'd expected it to be when she got to the office and before she knew it, she was at the front counter. Not long after that, she was back in her car with brand new stickers on her license plate. Job done, and 15 minutes to spare before it was Jane's normal time to leave.

And she'd met the mystery man again, she thought with a delighted smile. That was the best part of the whole outing. It meant he was still here, and if he was at the courthouse, maybe it meant he had moved to the small town. That made her smile even brighter, so bright that her face began to ache. She laughed at herself as she pulled into the driveway of her home and stopped the car.

Her mother might think all men were bad, and that they were only after one thing, but she wasn't her mother. She hadn't done all of the things her mother had done to get to the top, before her rather nasty fall from grace. She wasn't *that* kind of woman either. Men could want all they wanted to; it didn't mean she had to give it.

Her head tilted up in defiance as she walked up to the porch at the front of the house and opened the door. "I'm home, Jane."

"Oh, I thought you'd be another 45 minutes at least!" Jane said as she quickly walked into the living room. "You should have stayed out a little longer, Marie, taken a little bit of a break for yourself."

"I know you have a busy life too, Jane, but thank you. So, how much do I owe you for an hour and 15 minutes?" Marie pulled out her wallet, still with a smile on her face.

"Nothing, Marie, it was my pleasure to do it." Jane brushed the offer away, but Marie insisted.

"It's your time, Jane. Don't sell yourself short," Marie scowled gently. She wanted to say she wasn't a charity case but didn't because she might not be, but her mother was.

"I'm not, I just know how hard you work, all day long. It was my pleasure to help out, really. Keep your money." Jane pushed the wallet Marie held out away and gave Marie a no-nonsense look. "You deserve an hour or two here and there, you know?"

For the second time, Jane made Marie's

SUMMER COOPER

eyes well up, and she nodded her thanks as the woman gathered her things to leave. "Thank you, Jane. I mean that."

"I know you do, honey. I'll be back to-morrow." Jane headed for the door but paused once she had the screen door open. "This won't last forever, Marie. I'm not saying that to be cruel, but you need to know that. This won't last forever."

Jane emphasized the last word with a raised eyebrow and more weight in her voice. Marie took in a deep breath as the words sank in, and Jane left. She knew it wouldn't last forever, but to hear someone say it, that made it even more real for her. She was in a hard place, where her mother was concerned.

All of her life, she'd been tangled in her mother's web of hate and love. She'd always wanted to love her mother, and in a way she did. The woman gave her life and made a muddled attempt to keep her alive. The problem was, in between those muddled attempts, Ruby had made life hell for her.

There had been little in the way of affection when Marie was a child. Her mother would rather smack her than hug her. It had worked to keep Marie out of trouble, the fear of her mother's wrath, and those awful nights where she would rage until dawn, but they'd stripped Marie of most of the love she could have given the woman. A woman that obviously needed to be loved but wouldn't allow it.

Marie sat down on the faded couch, a pink monstrosity of faded fake velvet, and put her feet up on the coffee table. Her mother couldn't see her or she'd have never dared to put her feet there. Her whole life had been about fear, she realized, but it wouldn't last forever. Her mother's illness had progressed rapidly, and now, she was coming to a stage where she wouldn't last too much longer.

Sadness gripped her heart and squeezed it so tight Marie could barely breathe. The thought of her mother's imminent death hurt her, but it also gave her... hope. She hadn't quite allowed herself to think about that over the years. Her mother would be gone, and she would be free.

It felt like a betrayal to think that, but it was true. For all these years, she'd cared for, nurtured a woman that could barely stand the sight of her. Marie wasn't stupid, she knew her mother was a mean, vindictive woman that probably needed a psychiatrist, but it was too late now. Help might have come Ruby's way all those years ago when she came home, back to the small town her mother had been raised in. But, she'd felt herself above the hard-working and kind people of the town. She'd ruined her own reputation over and over again.

The community that so many others enjoyed here was lost to both Ruby and Marie through Ruby's actions. It wasn't just the drinking, there were plenty of women that got drunk on a Saturday night, out with their friends or a significant other. No, it had been her ranting, swearing, drunken rages, the affairs she'd had with other married men that had ruined any chance of help from their neighbors.

Marie was left to fend for herself, by most of the people of the town. Teachers at her school would sometimes bring her a sweater or make an extra sandwich for her, things they'd slip to her in her school bag, or when she was preparing to leave for the day. One of her teachers had even helped her to apply to universities, hopeful that Marie would flourish with her writing, but her mother had taken that from her.

As she'd taken everything. Even the clothes that were given to her, if she noticed that the clothes were something Ruby hadn't bought, that is. Most of the time she wouldn't notice, but when she did, Marie had to pay for it. Her mother would get out her belt, a special belt she'd bought just for whipping Marie with, and she'd strike at her own child with wild anger, screaming that it was Marie's fault for walking out of the house looking like a charity case.

When she was young, Marie believed

her mother. Everything was her fault, she was the reason her mother's career had ended, the reason her father died, the reason her mother had no friends. Over time, the truth became clear to Marie, however. It was her mother's fault, all of it.

Maybe it was her feelings of obligation, rather than love, that drove her now, she thought, as once again, her mother's voice filled the house with anger. Even in her current state, Ruby was angry. Angry at Marie, at the child she hadn't been able to get rid of. She could have given Marie up for adoption, but she hadn't. Marie had often wondered why.

She pulled on a pair of gloves and went back to her mother's room. She stood in the doorway and looked into the room, lit only by the machines around her mother's bed. Out of the semi-darkness, a croak of anger sent a shiver down her spine.

"Where have you been, you lazy slut? I've been calling you for hours now." The words were thick, forced out of a throat that didn't want to work.

"I've been here for an hour now, Mom. You just woke up." It was a common complaint, rather an accusation. She always accused Marie of bad things, mainly that she didn't take proper care of her.

Marie went to her mother, turned her body to the left, and pushed pillows down behind her to keep her on her side.

"I haven't just woken up I've been calling you." Ruby paused and worked up a little more energy to rasp out more words. "If you weren't so ugly and terrible, I'd say you were out with a man, but there's no man that would want a woman as lazy as you."

The words stung Marie and made her think of the mystery man she'd seen only a little while ago. He wanted her, she had seen it in his eyes. Interest mixed with something she knew instinctively was desire. Her mother's lies might still sting, but they no longer worked to convince her she was better off with Ruby.

"Never mind about men, Mom. Just get some rest." Marie checked the absorbent pads beneath her mother, and her clothing before she left the room.

If her mother hadn't been so cruel to her, she might have told her about the man, they might have been able to wonder together about who he was, what he did. But Ruby had always been cruel, and now, Marie kept the man a secret.

She wouldn't say anything about him, not to anyone. She might never see him again, but she doubted that. If he was at the courthouse today, he'd probably moved here. Which meant she would see him again, eventually. And hopefully, the people in town wouldn't warn him about her. Or her mother, more importantly.

If people told him about Ruby, he'd likely run away, never to be seen again. It would be one more thing Ruby took from her, even if she didn't know she had. Marie didn't know a lot about men, only what she'd seen on television, or learned through her own interactions with them. She knew what desire looked like, though, from the movies she'd seen. That was the look that was on his face earlier today, the mystery man. Desire. A man wanted her, and for the first time in her life, she felt that same desire. She just hoped it wasn't a misunderstanding.

5

Marie could tell from the smell of the meat-loaf in the oven that it was almost done. It wouldn't be long now, and she could finally have her dinner. She hummed along with the song on the radio, as she prepared instant mashed potatoes. They were quicker than peeling, boiling, and preparing the side dish, and she could measure out just enough for one person, then save the rest for the next time.

"Marie! I'm wet!" her mother croaked from the bedroom. Marie pulled her lips in between her teeth in frustration. IIer eyes stared blankly out the window over the sink as she stirred in milk and butter. A little salt and the dish was done.

She put the small ceramic bowl down on top of the stove so the heat from the oven would keep the potatoes warm, grabbed a pair of gloves, and headed back to her mother's room. She reconsidered the doctor's suggestion that they put a catheter into her mother, to stop the constant wetting. Marie was going to allow it until Jane told her how often her other patients developed urinary tract infections, which could cause delusions and other problems in bedbound, elderly patients.

She didn't need more problems to deal with and had refused the minor procedure. At times like now, when her dinner was barely done, she thought she'd made the wrong decision. Her mother had suddenly developed the problem, and at first, Marie had excused it as a new development in her mother's disease. Normally, she'd ask for the bedpan and use it, but then she started to have accidents. Marie had noticed that it seemed to happen most often when she was in the middle of doing something for herself. Cooking, bathing, sleeping, were all interrupted.

Marie had timed her mother's accidents once. She could go for hours without a single accident, but the minute Marie tried to do something for herself, her mother's bladder would let go. Or her bowels. That was even worse. Her little experiment, spread over a week, showed that the only time Ruby didn't call out for a bedpan was when Marie was busy. The rest of the time, she would be able to control her body's normal functions and would ask for the bedpan.

Marie had even tried doing these tasks at different times, just to see if it was a certain time of day, and she'd just correlated the two activities to each other. What she found was, it didn't matter if she took a shower at 5 pm or 9 pm, her mother had an accident. If she made her own breakfast at 9 am, or 11 am, her mother had an accident. If she went to sleep at 10 pm or 11 pm, her mother had an accident. Her experiment showed that it didn't matter what time Marie did something to take care of herself, her mother would have an accident. If Marie sat in the room the entire day without eating, bathing, or trying to sleep, her mother would ask for a bedpan.

These episodes of wetting herself, then, weren't accidents at all, but another effort to punish Marie. Marie knew all of this, knew that she had every right to hate her mother, but she couldn't. Not completely. She was angry with her mother and wanted things to be different, but she didn't hate her mother. Not exactly.

She gnawed at the inside of her cheek as she replaced the absorbent pads, wiped her mother down with extra-large wipes designed for adults, and replaced her nightgown. She could smell the acrid odor of her burning meatloaf over the scent of her mother's body and tried not to be upset.

Another burned dinner, but now her mother was dry at least. She turned her to her right side, checked her feet, and walked slowly to the kitchen. There was no need to run, after all, it wasn't going to be less burned if she did.

A strange calm had come over Marie when she walked into her mother's room. Jane's words from earlier in the day came back to her. It won't last forever. She'd looked down at the defiant gleam in her mother's eyes, at the way she'd smirked up at her daughter, and thought about the words. Soon enough, this would all be over. It didn't make her feel less angry, less abused, but it made her... calm.

She sat down to her burned dinner, slathered the meatloaf with ketchup, and slowly ate. She didn't want to wish her mother dead, and she didn't, but at the same time, she knew she couldn't go on much longer like this. She really did care about her mother, and always had, but she couldn't take much more.

Her life became even more meaningless when her mother's illness progressed rapidly. To the government, she was a caretaker and employee. To her mother's doctor, she was a caregiver, nothing more. To her mother, she was a slave. Jane had been the only person, or entity, that saw Marie as a person.

Marie was never asked how she was doing, and she rarely went to the doctor. Her mother was the sole focus of most of the people she interacted with. Nobody ever asked how the caretaker was, if the employee needed a break, a vacation that she never got to take. Nobody cared, except Jane.

Jane understood, but then she would, Marie thought. She did the same thing, only she did it for many patients, not just the one that Marie took care of. Jane saw how the daily practice of caring for patients wore down caregivers, though, and had sensed that Marie was nearing the end of her tether. Just that acknowledgment, that assurance that someone cared, was enough to make Marie emotional, even hours later. Her mouth flooded even as her eyes welled up with tears, all over again.

Someone had noticed her, had noticed the turmoil she tried to hide so much. Jane knew Ruby was a tyrant to her daughter. There was nothing Jane could do about it, but she could, and had, given Marie hope.

It wouldn't last forever.

Marie put her fork down and stared at the meatloaf left on her plate without actually seeing it. Jane wasn't the only person that had noticed Marie lately. That man with the car had too.

"Marie!" her mother shouted angrily. "What's taking you so long? My program will be on soon and you left the remote too far away for me to get it. Get in here, girl! What the hell is wrong with you?"

Marie sighed, stood up, and decided she wasn't that hungry anyway. Her mother had ruined her appetite.

"I don't know what you're doing in

there, instead of being in here taking care of me," her mother whined when she came into the room. "Always off doing something for yourself, never taking care of me. You want me dead, don't you? So you can run off with men and act like a whore."

"No, Mom, I don't," Marie whispered with resignation. "I was trying to eat my dinner."

"I'd like to eat dinner, but I have this fucking illness, don't I? I can barely swallow anything more than mush now, and I'm sick of it." Ruby pointed her crooked finger at Marie and gave her daughter an evil glare. "Lazy bitch, always eating. You'll end up fat, then no man will want you. As if one would want you now, anyway. Look at you, you haven't even put on makeup for crying out loud!"

The words stung, as they always did, but Marie tried to ignore it. That didn't work and the sting only spread through her chest which made her angry. "I don't really have time to do my hair or put on makeup, now do I, Mom?"

She couldn't help the words that slipped out. Her mother glared up at her, her eyes narrowed with suspicion. "Are you saying that's my fault? You could get up earlier, you know, make an effort."

Anger seethed inside of her as her mother's words echoed in her head. "Earlier? I'm up at 5 am on the days when you actually allow me to sleep for more than an hour at a time. If I get up any earlier, I wouldn't sleep at all!"

"That's your problem, not mine," her mother retorted, but her voice had grown scratchy. She wouldn't be able to talk soon, Marie knew, and couldn't wait for the enforced silence that would come. She could ignore her mother's hand gestures and angry eyes, but not her words. "It's not like any man would want you, even with makeup on. You're not much for anything, and you're just not beautiful. I thought you'd be much prettier, given the genes you had, but…"

The words trailed off into a croak, then nothing. Still, the anger inside of Marie grew and turned into something she couldn't control, a monster that would not be denied, for this one moment, at least.

"What do you know, Mom? Nothing really, because there is a man interested in me. And guess what? I'm interested in him too!"

"What?" Her mother's eyes became troubled, not with anger, but confusion. "What man?"

The words were little more than a whisper, but she managed to get them out.

"A very handsome, intelligent man, with a car, unlike anything I've ever seen. It's some old Lamborghini, so he must have money. I think he's Italian, but I haven't had time to ask him that, yet."

Her mother became agitated when she mentioned the car, and she even managed to almost push herself up in the hospital bed. Her hands clenched at the shiny rails so hard her arms quivered.

"He's not Mafia, is he? You stay away from Mafia men, girl. They're even more trouble than the rest of the men in the world. Cruel bastards, all of them." Ruby's anger made her throat work, but the voice was still little more than an angry whisper.

"I don't think he's Mafia, Mom. He's probably just some business mogul down here to get away from the city and the snow. He's not from around here, I know that, but I don't know anything about the Mafia, besides that garbage that goes on in New Orleans."

"I don't care who he is, or what he is really, girl. You stay away from him, you hear me? You gotta stay right here and take care of me, anyway. You don't have time for men or anything else. Just me!" Her mother's angry face twisted as she spoke, and Marie knew it took every ounce of energy her mother had to have her say.

It didn't matter though, not one bit. She

didn't care if her mystery man was Mafia or a vampire, for that matter. He brought something new and different into her life. There were possibilities, where before there'd been endless drudgery. The world had finally decided to pay her back for all the cruelty she'd endured over the years and had put the man in her path.

Maybe it was crazy, but she didn't care. The thought that he wanted to touch her, to hold her, to make her smile gave her hope, and she'd all but lost that in the last few months. Her mother's condition had become worse, and with each new symptom, Marie had lost more and more faith in the theory that we get what we give. Her faith was almost restored since she'd met him, though.

When she'd seen him for the second time, that faith had become a little firmer, a little more real. It didn't matter what her mother said to her, she knew, she knew deep down that she would do whatever she wanted with this man. She'd give him anything he asked for, as long as she had it to give.

"Mom, you wouldn't understand," Marie explained with quiet certainty. "You only ever took a man to bed because you wanted some material thing from him. You never took a man to bed to feel alive, to feel loved. If I ever go to bed with a man, that will be the only reason I do it. And you can't stop that. If I choose to sleep with this man, it's none of your business."

Marie's voice shook on the last sentence, but she got it out at least. For once, she'd stood up to her mother, and she felt the heady surprise of triumph as she stared down at her mother grimly. "This won't last forever, anyway."

Ruby's eyes went wide and she settled back down onto her pillows. Her left hand remained on the bed rail, gripped so tight Marie could see her mother's knuckles through the thin skin on her hands. She tried to say something, to rebuke Marie in some awful way, but she couldn't force the words out of her throat. That only made Marie's smile broader.

She felt a twinge of guilt, but pushed that down. It would do her mother some good to think things over, to know that her little punching bag/slave had taken more than enough. "You know, Mom. The reality is, you won't live forever. You really need to think about that. When you piss the bed to drag me out of the shower, or when you scream in one of your rages in the middle of the night, stop to think… you won't be alive forever, and maybe, just maybe, you should try to redeem yourself a little before that time comes."

Ruby's mouth worked, but it wasn't paralysis that made her speechless, it was Marie's words. Marie saw Ruby slide her head away, her eyes pained, and left the room at last. She didn't know if her words had any effect on her mother, but she hoped they did. Marie would love to have some emotion from her, other than the hate and anger she usually spewed at her daughter. Her memories would be wrapped in those emotions forever if her mother continued on this path, and that might be the saddest thing of all for Marie.

Marie came to terms with the fact that her mother was terminal a long time ago. What she hadn't considered was what would happen after her mother passed away. Jane had prompted her to see that, and now she wanted her mother to see it too. Ruby wouldn't be the queen of the bedroom forever.

Marie left her mother's room and went to her own. It was a plain room and always had been. A twin bed with a white coverlet on top, and white curtains in the room that was little more than a large broom closet. There was one white dresser and nothing more in the room.

Marie kept most of her clothes and shoes in the laundry room, though she didn't have many. Most of the clothes she did have were bought at a secondhand shop at the other end of the town a few years ago before her mother became bedridden. It was a good thing she hadn't gained any weight over the last few years. She couldn't afford 'new' clothes, and so she made do with what she had.

With a sigh of resignation, she sprawled out on her bed and stared up at the white ceiling. The walls were cheap pine sheets that had been nailed to the studs behind them. A very basic room, for a very basic girl. Woman, she thought after a moment. She was a grown woman now. And she'd just stood up to her mother for the first time in years.

She'd tried it when puberty hit when she was 12, and her hormones were all out of whack. Her mother had been nagging her about how she shouldn't become a whore now that she was able to make babies. She'd gone on and on about how she wasn't going to raise the kid if Marie got pregnant, and that she'd have to leave and marry the father if that happened. If he wasn't already married.

That had been the part where Ruby crossed a line and Marie had jumped up from the same table in the kitchen that was there now and screamed at her mother, "You're the whore in this family. You're the one that fucks married men, Momma, not me!"

Ruby became enraged and dragged Marie to the floor by her hair and slapped her face until her nose began to bleed. "You don't ever mention those things to me, do you understand little girl? Never, ever backtalk me or try to put me down."

Each word had been punctuated with another slap and a harder tug at Marie's hair. She'd given in, so the pain of her hair being ripped from her head would stop. She'd felt really bad about insulting her mother, too, and hadn't tried it again. Not until today anyway. Today, she'd succeeded at last. Her mother hadn't been able to hit her this time, and that was one step closer to freedom.

6

The next morning, Ruby was ill. Well, more ill than usual. She was almost delirious when Marie got up. A quick check of her temperature showed that the bedridden woman had a fever. Marie's gut clenched and she felt shame for her outburst the day before. Her mother was right to be angry; her life had been hard. And Marie had only made that life harder.

She still felt like her mother should be nicer to her, and she still wanted her freedom, but she felt bad about it. The woman was her mother and deserved respect for that at least. Marie smoothed her mother's short white hair down and felt pity for her. It was something she hadn't felt in a long time.

Jane's statement had started a chain reaction, but Marie's actions after the statement were what really counted. She'd been... not nice to her mother.

"I'm sorry I was mean to you yesterday, Momma. I'll call Jane and see what she thinks we should do."

Ruby mewled in her sleep and grasped at Marie's hand tightly. Marie tried to tug her hand away, but Ruby wouldn't let go. *"Je t'aime, Maman."*

Marie froze. Ruby rarely spoke about her mother, other than to say she'd been famous in the late 60s and early 70s. Something had happened, Ruby never did know what, but it drove the starlet back to Louisiana to hide in the swamps. There'd been a lot of money, so they'd had a nice house, and servants, things that Ruby couldn't afford.

Marie had learned over the years that her mother didn't want Ruby to go into movies, but Ruby had ignored her warnings. She'd done what she wanted to do and faced the consequences. The woman had been remarkable according to Ruby. She'd spoken English, Cajun French, and Spanish. She'd made movies in Italy, Saudi Arabia, America, and England. By all accounts, she was an intelligent, beautiful woman that had been incredibly talented.

Ruby had been on her way to that kind of stardom when she'd wound up pregnant with some Mafia guy's baby. It had destroyed her career and her life. It had made her bitter and twisted in ways that Marie still couldn't understand. Now, as her mother held her hand and whispered to her long-dead mother, Marie felt empathy, more than pity. Her mother had broken all the rules and paid the price for it. Now she was bedridden, unable to escape even the pain that came with her disease.

Marie took a deep breath and reached

for the small, cheap cell phone. They couldn't afford smartphones, computers, or the internet, but she did have a cheap cell phone if she needed help. She called Jane and asked her to come early. She was there in less than 15 minutes.

She came into the bedroom with a solemn look. "Let's have a look at her. I spoke to the doctor, he's ordered a urine sample, so we'll have to find a way to get some out of her if she doesn't wake up. I suspect she has a UTI."

"But I thought she wouldn't get them if she didn't have the catheter?" Marie's brows knit in confusion as she looked down at her mother. "I'm so careful when I wash her and make sure I go front to back every time she's had... an accident."

"You can be as careful and as sterile as you can be, Marie, sometimes the infections happen anyway." Jane put her hand over Marie's arm on the bed rail. Marie looked down at the hand then back up at Jane.

"It's not my fault?" Marie asked, her voice hopeful.

"More than likely not, Marie. These things happen with bedridden patients. It can't always be helped." Jane patted her arm and went about collecting a sample of urine from Ruby.

Marie turned her mother onto her back and held her there, though Ruby really didn't protest at all. Jane used a catheter to collect the urine sample that she needed while Marie watched. The process made her cringe because she knew that the catheters felt like a rough pipe cleaner being shoved into her urethra. She'd had a lot of UTIs as a child, and she'd had to be catheterized once. She could still remember the sensations of it, the way it felt like an invasion. She shuddered and looked away.

"I'll take the sample to the lab and if there are any signs of infections I'll bring back some antibiotics for her." Jane put the sample in a plastic bag, sealed the bag, and put it in her carrying case.

"Thanks, Jane, that would be great." Marie sat down in the chair at her mother's bedside and picked up her right hand. "She's all I have, you know?"

Marie wasn't sure if she wanted Jane to know that or herself. When she'd gone to sleep last night, she'd felt so triumphant, like she'd won a lifelong battle. Now, with her mother delirious and ill, she didn't feel so big anymore. She felt small and helpless, as she always did.

What would happen to her when her mother was gone? It was a question that needed an answer. She knew the house and car would be hers, so she'd have a place to live, but after that? Where would she work? The only job she'd ever had was as her mother's personal care assistant. Would that count? She'd undergone training to get the job, so maybe it would?

She chewed at a plastic floss stick after lunch later that day as she pondered the question. She went back to the job of flossing and stared off into nothing. There were a lot of elderly people in town that might need her care, but would they want her in their house?

It was a possibility, but maybe she could drive to nearby towns, where they didn't know her? Something would come up, surely?

A knock at the back door told her Jane was back. The screen door opened, and the other woman came in. They rarely used the front door and Marie spent most of her time not at her mother's beck and call in the kitchen. Jane was such a familiar person at the house now that Marie no longer expected her to knock. "Hey, you had to come back, that's not good then?"

It came out breathy and frightened. A UTI would be easy to treat but it could turn into something worse for those that were unable to move around. Staying in bed like that seemed to lower the immune system and wreaked havoc in so many ways. Part of Jane's daily duties were moving Ruby's arms and legs, to keep the blood flowing and try to give her even that little bit of exercise. Ruby didn't always comply, but it helped.

"The doctor wanted to put her on an IV drip, which I may have to do if she won't wake up and take these pills." Jane handed a white paper bag over to Marie and gave her the instructions. "If she doesn't take them, we'll have to put in an IV. Or if she gets worse, of course."

Jane sat down at the table her face etched with weariness. She put her elbows on the table and her head in her hands. "It's so hot outside, how can you two stand it?"

"I guess we're used to it." Marie glanced at the fan on the kitchen counter and thought about her Mom's AC unit. It was the only room that was ever cool, even if the door was open. "It's only bad because it's going to storm. Once that passes it'll cool off a little."

"You hope. We all know how the weather is here. Hot and soaking wet, hot and damp, or hot. I swear, I almost melted on the way from the car into here." Jane smiled as if the thought amused her. "I almost started to say that line about I'm melting, but didn't."

Marie knew she meant a line from the Wizard of Oz. It used to come on television when she was a child, and she remembered it well. "I could just imagine you doing that."

"I need to get back out in it now," Jane said suddenly and stood up. "You have my number. Call me if she gets worse, or you need a hand getting her to take the medicine."

"I will, Jane, and thanks. You're too good to us." Marie leaned in to peck Jane on the cheek and the other woman simply smiled as she offered her cheek.

"You deserve all the help you can get, Marie, don't doubt that." She squeezed Marie's shoulders and then left.

Marie sighed heavily and then turned to face the doorway that would take her to her mother's room. She'd make her mother some gumbo, something soft and simple, she'd like that. Marie started the soup-like meal, and then went back to her mother with a glass of cranberry juice. It took some doing, but she managed to wake her up.

"What do you want, Marie? I don't feel well. Go to school, already, and leave me alone."

Marie felt a chill run down her spine when her mother said the oh so familiar words. Words she'd heard so many times as a child, in need of money for lunch or sick herself and in need of care. Now, she was the one doing the caring, and she had to be strong. Firm, certainly, but gentle too. She wanted her mother to know, from now on, that she would not be spoken to like a slave. But that was for when her mother recovered. Right now, she needed to take her medicine.

"Take these, Mom, they'll help." Marie had added ibuprofen to take away some of the swelling and pain. It was also the doctor's orders to do so.

"I can't take all of those at once," Ruby moaned at her daughter but took the pills. With a look of defiance, she threw the pills in her mouth, took the bottle of water Marie offered her, and swallowed. "There."

Marie smirked with amusement when her mother stuck her tongue out and moved it around to show she'd swallowed the pills. Sometimes, not often, but every now and then, her mother's rebellious streak made her laugh. "Good girl."

"What's for dinner? Is that gumbo?" Ruby looked up at Marie suspiciously. "You only make me that when I'm ill."

"But you are ill, Mom. Very ill. Now lie back and let me check your skin." Marie grabbed a pair of gloves and examined her mother's skin once again, and soon found everything to be fine. "Good, relax now. I'll bring the gumbo in when it's done."

"Thank you." Ruby looked as surprised as Marie felt. Had her mother actually thanked her?

"You're welcome, Mom," Marie uttered

before she went through the doorway and into the dark hall covered with a dark shade of green carpet. The carpet ran into most of the rooms in the house, except for the kitchen and Marie's room. Marie preferred the bare floors to the carpet and had taken it up when she was a teenager. With her mother's permission, of course.

She added a few things to the gumbo, checked the flavor, and then sat down with a book to read as she listened to the radio. Her mother would be asleep in minutes, so she settled down to let the food cook.

She liked to read anything, but lately, she'd started to read thrillers. They kept her on the edge of her seat and gave her an opportunity to live an exciting life, that was, well, thrilling. Her life was so boring and mundane, sometimes awful, and the books helped her to escape into a new life that she could never imagine on her own.

A smell filled the air, one that Marie was all too familiar with. Her mother had an accident. And not one that she could wipe away with a single wipe either. The smell was terrible, and by the time she'd finished cleaning up the mess, a mess her mother couldn't help, she no longer felt like eating.

Her mother did, though, so she made her a bowl, and fed it to her. By the time the bowl was empty, her mother was asleep again. Marie took a shower, put on a clean nightgown, and went to bed without dinner. She'd put the gumbo in the fridge, and she'd have it for lunch tomorrow. Tonight, her stomach wasn't interested in eating at all.

7

"Why is it so hot in here?" Jane inquired as she came into Ruby's bedroom.

"The air conditioner died last night, and I don't have the money to get a new one. Even if I did have the money, I couldn't leave her to go buy one." Marie had been fanning her mother with a paper fan she'd made but stopped now that Jane was there. "I brought the fan in, but Mom's still sweating. I don't think those antibiotics are working."

"It's only been a couple of days, let's give it a little while longer," Jane said thoughtfully as she moved closer to the bed. "I might know someone that has an extra air conditioner they don't need. Let me ask them while you're gone, and if they'll let you have it, I'll bring it by later on."

"Really? That would be so... wonderful!" Marie's smile was almost beatific as she beamed at Jane. "I've been so worried about her all night long, I barely slept."

"Well, go out, relax for a little bit, and don't worry. I'll see if we can get this sorted." Jane's reassurance that all was under control eased Marie's mind.

Throughout the night she'd panicked over the fact that her mother didn't seem to be improving, and the fact that the air conditioner wouldn't work. She'd tried and tried but couldn't figure out what was wrong with the machine that simply refused to come on. She'd finally given up, brought in the fan from her room, and made another fan out of paper to wave over her mother. It wasn't much, but it was better than nothing.

Marie got up from the chair that had once been covered in a red velvet-like material but was now faded and patched. It was a soft, comfortable chair, and Marie refused to give it up for that reason. It made the hours she spent at her mother's bedside a little more comfortable, why should she replace it?

"I'll go clean up and head out for a bit. Thanks, Jane." Marie brushed her fingers over Jane's shoulder in gratitude as she walked out.

A short while later, she was seated at the café with a cup of café au lait, her beignets, and a book. She was too tired to read, and the way the sun slanted on the pages made it a chore to see the words, but she tried because it was one of her favorite things to do. Today, she didn't have to go to the store or pick up a prescription, all she had to do was relax. Only she couldn't.

Her mother's condition weighed on her like a 2-ton weight. What would she do if her mother didn't improve? She felt like a yo-yo, being pulled by a child that had never pulled one before. She was jerked in one direction only to be thrown in another direction before she was jerked back into the same direction. Then she just sort of flailed around, with no direction at all. Which was where she was right now. She had no idea what to do, or who to talk to. There was always Jane, but she felt bad for burdening the woman with her problems.

It was great that Jane might be able to get an air conditioner for her mother, but at the same time, Marie felt bad about it. She was her mother's daughter, she should be able to provide for her. It hurt her pride, just a little, that she couldn't just go out and buy a new AC unit.

"May I join you?" A deep male voice, accented with that Yankee sound, drew Marie's gaze upward.

It was him!

Her jaw dropped a little and she looked around as if to make sure he was talking to her. "I, uh, yes, if you'd like."

"I would like to. My name is Matteo, by the way. Matteo Mazza." He put down his coffee and beignets and sat down across from her at the little white table with white chairs. He held his hand out and she felt her face turn red.

"Marie Hebert." She took his hand and felt the touch as a buzz of electricity. His hand was so warm, big, and comforting. Like he'd taken on her problems and he'd fight the world for her. His eyes were different though, they devoured her, from head to toe, with a hunger that she couldn't ignore.

She stared into those eyes, unable to look away. She forgot how to breathe, to let his hand go, and they sat at the table, frozen in that moment as their hands touched. Then, he blinked and let her hand go.

"Sorry, forgot myself for a moment there. I see you've mastered the problem of dressing in this incredible heat." His head nudged in the direction of her body.

She'd worn a pair of denim shorts, a

lacy, cotton, white blouse, and her ever-present flip flops. She looked at him and frowned. In contrast, he had on a pair of dark denim jeans that looked like they were made from a thick material, the kind she thought of as winter jeans, rather than the thinner material of summer jeans. Along with that he had on a white Oxford shirt with the sleeves rolled up, and on his feet were a pair of leather loafers. Way too many clothes.

Then she blushed again because she'd suddenly imagined him naked. "It's alright, you'll learn to adapt. Down here, even senators wear shorts sometimes."

"I bet they do. I wanted to come down here for a change of scenery and knew it was hot but damn. This is incredible."

"It is. Wait until the mosquitoes start. Even with the mosquito abatement programs, we still get them."

"It's amazing down here, I love everything about it, but you've just mentioned the two things I hate. Mosquitos and heat."

"Well, we have plenty of both of those down here." Marie looked at him with amused glee. It felt easy talking to him like it was something they'd done many times before. She also noticed the way his lips moved when he bit into a beignet or took a sip of his coffee. She noted the strength in his hands, but the delicacy with which he picked up his coffee cup. Sensual was the word that sprang to mind. He was a sensual man. Even the smell of his cologne was... sensual.

Something warm, languid, and giddy tensed in her lower abdomen as she watched him eat. She'd never been so totally *aware* of a man before. There were plenty of men in town that could draw her eyes, but she'd never been interested in them. Not like she was this man.

"Is it better in the winter?" he asked once he'd finished eating. He wiped his fingers on a napkin and she was almost jealous of the thing when he wiped his mouth with it.

She pulled her bottom lip in between her teeth to stop herself from saying something stupid like… "take me away forever, you sex-god". When the urge had passed, she spoke. "Oh, a little bit. It has actually snowed a time or two. None of it really stuck to the ground, but it has been known to snow."

"Really? I bet the kids around here loved that. It's so common where I'm from, we only see it as a nuisance. Well, we adults do. I have a feeling the kids don't. It gets them out of school, right?" His smile fascinated her. It brightened his face and lit up his eyes in a way that tugged at her heart.

"I wouldn't know, really." She realized what she'd said, what she'd all but admitted, and cleared her throat. "I'm usually at home taking care of my mother so I don't see many people most of the time."

"Oh?" His brows knit together, and he leaned in towards her. "What do you mean? Is your mother ill?"

"Yes, she's in the last stage of Parkinson's

disease. I'm her main caretaker. There's a nurse that comes in for an hour a day so I can run errands. Every now and then I get to do this." She paused to point at the coffee and book. "It's not often, but every now and then, I have the time to sit here for a little while."

"It sounds rough. An hour a day to yourself? That's almost... prison." His face revealed his thoughts. Horror at being so trapped, then compassion and understanding. "She's your mother, though. You're a good daughter."

"I try to be." Marie looked away, she didn't want to see pity on his face.

"I guess that means I can't ask you out for dinner one night, then?" The lilt of hope in his voice made her heart flutter.

"Um. No," she staggered out her response, because she really wanted to accept, but knew she couldn't. She could ask him to dinner at her house, but no. She didn't want him to see the state of the place. It was clean and tidy, but it was obvious they were poor. She didn't want him to see that. "I do have another idea, though. If you'd like to see me again."

"Oh?" His left eyebrow quirked and a grin stretched out his features. "Do tell?"

"I might be able to make it here tomorrow, for a little while." She halted, unsure for a moment. Did she dare? But then, she looked up to see his eyes alive with happiness. "For a little while."

"I'll take what I can get," he offered with an amused look. "And you'll know you'll be safe, it's a public place."

"Oh, it's not that at all," she rushed to assure him. "I just don't have a lot of free time. Especially now. My mother has another illness and it's exacerbated the problems she already had."

Marie didn't want to say that she'd been depressed when he showed up but knew her voice revealed her unhappiness. That compassionate look came back, and he nodded his head.

"I understand, Marie. It's tough having a

parent so ill. I won't nag you about anything. I'll just be happy with whatever time you can give me."

"Thank you." She glanced at her watch, always aware of the time when she was away from home. "Unfortunately, I have to go. I didn't realize how long I've been here trying to read this book."

He glanced down at the book, noted the title, and looked impressed. "Thrillers, I like that."

"Good," she said with a laugh of appreciation. "I'm kind of stuck on this author. They're old books, but I like them. They're full of ghosts and wickedness. And I can read the whole collection now, they've been around for a long time."

"Yes, I liked them too, when I read them." He nodded as if to agree with himself.

She was surprised he read. For some reason, it had never occurred to her that men really would sit down and read a book. Of course, she hadn't been around a lot of men in her life, outside of school and the business she had to take care of. It just didn't seem like something a man would do to her. The fact that he did read impressed her even more than the car or the display of wealth in his personal attire. The ring he wore on his right middle finger was probably worth more than her yearly income alone. That didn't count the necklace or the watch he had on.

She glanced at his right wrist and noted the faint creep of jet-black ink. She couldn't tell what the tattoo was, and when his arm moved, she quickly looked away. She didn't want to admit that it gave him a bad boy air, that tattoo. She fought to keep a pleased smile off of her face. She liked everything about the man so far.

She'd never really thought about what type of man she would like to have she'd never thought that far ahead into the future. Now, she knew exactly what her type was. Him.

"I guess I'll see you tomorrow, then? You

can fill me in on all the local secrets and skeletons that await in people's closets." The happy smirk on his face did things to her that she didn't understand, but she liked it.

"I might just do that," she finally uttered, her ability to speak all but forgotten. "I'll, uh, yeah. I'll see you tomorrow." She gave him a nod and stood up to leave. "I hope you won't be disappointed if I can't make it. Sometimes I'm delayed, and can't help it."

"I understand. Why don't you take my card and if you can't meet me, just let me know? We'll set up another day." He pulled out his wallet, took out a business card, and gave it to her.

"That's a good idea, I don't know why I didn't think of that." She took the card, looked down at it, and saw it was on cardstock that must have been very expensive. "Thank you."

"I'll see you soon, Marie. Take care of yourself." He gave a short wave from his chair and she tried not to fall over as she walked to her car. She was so happy she wanted to jump for joy or fall over with re-lieved excitement. A man wanted to take her on a date! And not just any man, Matteo Mazza. Even his name was sensual.

She repeated it to herself as she drove home, still full of giddy hope. She didn't hear the radio or the way the tires changed sounds as she drove over asphalt and then cement, and then asphalt again. All she heard was the sound of his voice as he told her goodbye. He'd been very pleased she'd agreed to meet him, and that was some-thing she thought she'd never get to hear. The thought was dimmed, however, when she drew near to the driveway. In that house was her mother.

In an instant, everything fell down around her as she realized she'd never have time to date him. That he'd get tired of her eventually because she didn't know how to pluck her own eyebrows or have the money for makeup and haircuts. He'd want a proper woman at some point, and she couldn't be that.

Even if her mother didn't drain all of her paychecks, she still couldn't afford to buy the kinds of clothes a man like Matteo would expect his woman to wear. Expensive things that she didn't even have a clue where to buy. Where did you buy clothes from Louis Vuitton or other designers? She had no idea, and that made the frown on her face deepen a little more.

Who was she kidding, she thought? She couldn't date a man like Matteo. She wasn't his kind.

8

Marie woke up the next morning and stared up at her ceiling. She'd pushed her thin blanket off during the night, and the breeze from her fan blew her hair out of her face. Did she go and meet Matteo, or did she let him go? If she did it now, she wouldn't know the pain that would come later, when he figured out that she wasn't good enough for him.

A loud bang from her mother's room got her out of bed, and she went in to see what was wrong. Her mother was there, her hair a wild halo around her head, anger spewing from her eyes. She was trying to speak, but words wouldn't come out.

"What's wrong, Mom?" Marie asked, and watched as her mother put her hands between her legs. "Ah, the bedpan. Just a second."

Marie went into the bathroom, put on a pair of gloves, and grabbed the bedpan. With practiced movements, she put the pan under her mother and turned away. After a few minutes, Marie was about to turn around when something hit her in the back of the head. She knew what it was the second warm liquid poured down her hair and back.

Her mother had thrown the used bedpan at her.

She took a deep breath, turned around to see that there'd only been urine in the bedpan, thankfully, and cleaned her mother up. Her mother struggled with her the entire time and slapped Marie in the face twice. Marie ignored both slaps, but when her mother clawed her short nails down Marie's arm, she cried out with pain.

Blood welled along the length of the scratches and Marie looked at her mother with horrified anger. "Mom! What the hell?"

Her mother just glared at her angrily. Marie wanted to tell her mother off, wanted to make her pay somehow, deep down inside she felt the need to hit out angrily, but she controlled it. Her mother couldn't help this. Her mother was an invalid. Her mother didn't deserve the life she'd had.

It played like a mantra in her mind as she finally got her mother cleaned up and situated in the bed. It was only then that she went in to take a shower. Her mother's needs were always the priority for her, even if that meant she had to clean up the woman with urine dripping from her hair and down her back. Once she'd showered, she went back into the bedroom to clean the carpet.

That took a lot of effort as the urine had soaked in, but in the end, she was certain she'd cleaned it all up. She looked at the scratches on her arm, three lines that were already scabbing over. At least there were no bruises on her face, she thought before she got up and went into the kitchen. She took out the medicines her mother needed to take, prepared her breakfast, and took it into her on a tray.

Ruby promptly threw the hot oatmeal and scrambled eggs at Marie and the wall. The pills she picked up and tossed behind the bed. It all happened before Marie could stop her, and she stood shocked as the oatmeal dripped down her face. The oatmeal wasn't hot enough to really burn her, but it was still warm and could have burned her if it had been a little hotter. She pulled the bed tray from her mother's lap so she couldn't throw that, and ran into the bathroom to wash the oatmeal from her hair.

Marie stared at herself in the mirror once her hair and face were cleaned up. She looked like what she was: a nervous wreck. Ruby had been hard to handle before this infection, but now? Now she was a holy terror and Jane would have to do something. There had to be something that the doctor could give her to make that infection go away!

By the time Jane walked into the house, Marie had changed tops again and cleaned up the floor of the eggs and oatmeal.

Marie was just about to walk back to try to get her mother to take her medicine again when Jane walked in.

"Hi! How is she today?" Jane asked in a cheery, hopeful voice.

"Terrible!" Marie sobbed and started to cry. "I don't think I can do this anymore, Jane. I just... my God, how much am I supposed to take?"

The older woman took Marie into her arms and soothed her. "Tell me what's wrong?"

Marie relayed the events of the morning to Jane and explained how she was exhausted. "I'm just tired, Jane. I've been doing this for years now, and it's only getting worse. Which, I mean, I knew that would happen, but I had no idea she'd attack me like this."

"It happens sometimes when they have infections. Listen, I'll call the doctor and ask him about admitting her to the hospital. That would give you a couple of days to regroup."

"Do you think he would?" Marie hiccupped, the tears drying up as hope flooded into her.

"He might," Jane stressed the last word with a sigh. "He needs to, just to give you a break. You go on out, I'll get her medicine down her, and check her over. I'll see you in an hour, alright?"

Marie looked down at the beige shorts she had on and the gray tank top. Not what she would have chosen to wear out to meet Matteo, but it was what she had on. A need to escape the house, and her mother, drove her to run for her purse and the car keys.

She sprinted to the car and sped out of the driveway like demons were chasing her and she had to escape.

In her mind, she was escaping demons, well, her mother, and she wanted out as fast as she could get. She loved her mother, in the best way that she could. She loved the woman, out of respect for her position as her mother, but sometimes... sometimes she really didn't like the woman at all.

She carried a lot of guilt about that, but there had never been anyone to tell her that her mother was a bitch that needed a good dose of reality about what life was like. Marie had often had those kinds of thoughts, but nobody had ever said that was normal to her. Because of that, she felt terribly guilty.

She drove into town with the radio off, hoping the road noise would soothe her, would let her brain calm down a little. Her cheek wasn't bruised, but it was still red, and she could swear she could still smell the faint odor of pee in her hair.

Marie wanted to stop the car on a quiet stretch of the road and cry, but she'd promised Matteo she'd meet him, and after this morning, she needed the sunshine his presence brought to her life. She needed the way he made her feel when she was with him. She craved his attention, that feeling of safe contentment, that she had when he was near her. She barely knew him, but already, she wanted him in her life. Now, she just had to find a way to meet with him more often, all while she figured out how she'd convince him she wasn't damaged goods, or not worthy of him.

Her foot pressed down harder on the gas pedal and her fingers tightened on the wheel. Right now, she wanted to focus only on him. Later, she'd worry about what to do with her mother. Hopefully, Jane would succeed with the doctor, and her mother would take a nice long trip to the hospital.

The idea didn't please her because she thought she'd get time with a man, but more because she wouldn't have to deal with a woman that abused her. She was trapped with that woman for 23 hours a day. It was hard enough when she wasn't delirious, but now? It was too much to take.

As she pulled into a space in front of the café, Marie made a decision. She would not talk about how pitiful her life was, she wouldn't whine about her position. She'd just talk with him, get to know him, and hopefully, she'd be able to deflect most of the questions he was bound to have if they involved her mother.

"Hi," she called out brightly when she spotted him at the same table they'd used the day before. "Did you even leave the place?"

She knew he had because he had on a pair of black shorts and a thin white t-shirt that fit loosely around his chest. Not as sexy as those tight shirts he wore, but she didn't mind. The heat down there could kill a person.

"Nope, been here since yesterday after-noon waiting on you." He grinned at her, and she could swear her knees went weak. She sat down across the table from him and smiled weakly.

"Persistent, aren't you?" She meant it as a joke, but he nodded his head seriously.

"I am. You're a lovely woman, and you have this gentle air about you. I like it." He smiled, amused at himself. "It doesn't hurt that you're beautiful."

"Oh," she said and brushed at her hair with her fingers. "I'm glad you think so."

"I do, but that's not why I'm here. You're the most interesting person I've met since I've been here." He leaned forward as he spoke. "Most people have greeted me with a southern charm that oozes right out of them, but you've just been… normal, I guess is the right word."

"You just don't know," Marie said with a laugh and a slight wave of her hand. "The women here will mother you to death if you let them. And the men? Well, another pool-playing beer buddy never hurt any-one, right?"

Marie hadn't known an ounce of love or support from the community over the years, except for her teachers, but otherwise, there'd been no one that cared for her the way she'd just described to Matteo. She'd seen it with other people and had felt a niggle of resentment over it. Nobody cared about her like that. Nobody gave two fucks if she lived or died. She wasn't here for complaining, though, so she turned her thoughts away.

"But why don't they do the same to you? Why aren't there armies of women lined up at your door to help?"

"Well, that's a long story. They help in their own ways." Marie evaded the question. "Last night we were given a new air conditioner by one lady if that tells you anything."

Marie hoped it was enough to end that line of questioning. She wasn't very good at this evasion game with him and knew she'd give something away if she wasn't careful. His eyes seemed to draw out the honesty in her, and it felt wrong to not be completely honest with him.

"It does, actually. It tells me a lot." Matteo nodded his head and looked around at the café doors. "You want something? I'll run in and get it. I know you don't have a lot of time to be here and you should stay off your feet for a while. You look tired today."

He didn't know the half of it, she thought as he walked into the café to get her usual order. The woman inside knew what Marie wanted, she'd been there often enough, and Matteo soon came out with her drink and a plate of beignets.

"That will perk you up," he said as he put the items on the table and sat down.

"I hope so. I'm sorry if I look bad. It was… a rough morning."

"Don't worry about it, you're still the most beautiful woman I've ever seen." The way he said it made her almost believe him.

She knew she wasn't ugly. Her mother's mix of Spanish and French genes, along with her father's Italian, had produced a child that was alright to look at. She thought her nose was too big for her face and that her ears stuck out too far from her head, but he didn't seem to notice that.

"I think the local beauty queens would disagree with you, but I'm glad you think so." She brushed his fingers with hers, a move that surprised her, but she was glad she did it. Awareness became a thing she finally understood as he looked at her. She'd read about it in books but had no idea what it really meant.

Now, as her skin went tight and every cell of her body seemed to draw towards him, she knew exactly what it meant. She was aware of him in ways she'd never been aware of a person before. It was an incredible thing to experience and all she could do was look at him, helpless to do anything but that.

He snapped out of it first and sat back. He still looked at her, but the odd moment had passed. He smiled, easily, as if comfortable with what had just taken place. "I like you, Marie. I don't know why, but I really do."

"Good. I like you too." She glanced down at his arm, the one with the tattoo, and saw what it was now. His name, in cursive letters, going up from his lower wrist to his elbow. There were smaller, finer things entwined with the letters, leaves maybe? She couldn't tell and didn't want to stare.

"So, what do you do for fun around here?" he asked. A perfectly innocent question, but one she wasn't sure how to answer.

"I guess that depends on what you consider fun?" She asked it as a question, to avoid answering right away.

"A good meal, some exercise, boating, um," he gave a bashful smile and scratched at the back of his head with an index finger. "I don't know, what do you guys do?"

"Lots of things, boating on the river or out in the spillway. Swimming in the lake or drive down to the Gulf. There are bars, dance halls, and I think there might even be an illegal strip club or two, out in the backwoods." It was a rumor she'd heard many times, as she sat in waiting rooms, so still, people would forget she was even there.

"Nah, those don't interest me. What about films? Theater? You got anything like that?"

"Up towards New Orleans, yeah. Down this way, on the outskirts, not so much. I can take you out in the bayou, show you huge snakes, spiders, and bats if you'd like."

"Could you indeed?" He looked intrigued.

"If my mom didn't need me I would." She pulled her lip between her teeth, for the billionth time in her life, and tried to think of what to say next. "I don't know how long that will be, Matteo. You should know that. It might be that I can only give you an hour every now and then for a long time. Or it might not be. I don't know."

"I'll take what you can give me." He

leaned back, comfortable under the umbrella at the table. "I've got time."

"I'm glad one of us does." She took a final sip of her coffee and glanced at her watch. "I can't believe it's that time already! I have to go. I'm so sorry, but I'll be late if I don't go now."

"It's fine, I'll see you again soon. Just text me, alright?" He gave her a wide smile, held out his hand, and when she gave hers to him, he pulled her closer to him. "I have all the time in the world for you, sweetheart. Don't worry so much, alright?"

She gasped but nodded, as his lips came down. She held her face up to him, wanted him to kiss her lips, but instead he brushed his lips against the side of her cheek. Somehow, that was better than a kiss on the lips. She pulled back to look up at him, completely befuddled.

"Drive home carefully, alright? You're precious cargo." He winked as she stood up and left.

The grin on her face couldn't be

dimmed, even when she got home and found out the doctor wouldn't admit her mother to the hospital.

"Maybe when she yanks her IV out and bleeds all over, he'll realize she needs to be hospitalized. Until then, call me if you need me, honey." Jane was in a hurry to leave and Marie knew her mother was still being a terror. She sighed and went into the bedroom her mother occupied, but even the glare of hate her mother sent her way couldn't dim the warmth in her chest or the way she felt, deep down inside. She was... happy.

9

"I can't believe a month has passed already," Marie whispered to herself as she got dressed to meet with Matteo. She said it out loud, even though there was no one to hear her because she had to make it real. Thinking it didn't seem to make the fact a fact, so she tried saying it out loud.

It helped, and she smiled as she slipped into an old but still wearable pink dress. She'd bought it for her high school graduation and hadn't worn it since. She was amazed it still fit and smoothed the panels down with careful hands. It was an A-line dress, cut into panels that had been stitched together, with a deep V at the top. The skirt went down to her calves and was more respectable than the top.

It wasn't exactly out of fashion and it was a more mature dress than she'd have bought back then, but she'd felt like a grown-up, so she'd bought it. She liked the way the material swirled around her upper legs. It was a classic dress and to Marie, it was classy. Her mother had even said so when she saw it. Even if she had ruined the moment by telling Marie not to act like a trollop at the graduation ceremony just because she was out of school now.

Marie rolled her eyes at the memory and went about finishing her getting ready process. That meant putting her hair up in a ponytail and making sure her fingernails weren't jagged or dirty. She had no idea how to style her hair and had no makeup. She didn't have to do a lot to get ready. She was clean, not sweating yet, and presentable.

She slipped her feet into a pair of her mother's old black stilettos, the only fancy shoes she had, and went into the living room. Her mother was asleep, so the woman Jane had arranged for waited in there for Marie to come out. The woman was from another town and Marie didn't know her, but she had only asked for $20 to watch her mother for two hours, and Jane recommended her. It was worth giving up her favorite snack for a week or two to go on this date with Matteo.

Over the last month, they'd spent every hour they could together, and he'd asked her if she could arrange for two hours, in the evening, so she could go have dinner at his house. She'd agreed, and now, she was ready to go.

"Jane's explained everything right? And you have my number?" Marie asked the woman. Carol, that was her name!

"Yes, honey. You go on now, we'll be fine. You deserve a break from what Jane said, so you go on now, *cher*." Only, when the woman said *cher*, the old French word for dear or darling, it came out as *sha*. Marie smiled at the endearment and thanked the woman.

"I'll be back by 9. I promise, no dilly-dallying."

"Take your time, *cher*. I'll be right here taking care of your momma for ya, go on now."

Marie finally left and picked up the directions Matteo wrote down for her. She thought she knew where the house was, but like the bayou, some of the houses around went deep back into the woods and were hidden away from view. She wasn't as familiar with some of those places, despite living in the town for all of her life.

She knew she'd found it when she spotted a discrete fence with one of those ornate steel gates in the middle that slid away to allow a car through. There was a box just in front of the gate where she stopped and pressed a button.

"May I help you?" a bored voice came out of the speaker in the box.

"Uh, hi, yes. I'm Marie Hebert, here to see Matt... er, Mr. Mazza please."

"Just a moment, Ms. Hebert, I'll open the gate for you." The speaker went quiet. A new sound came as the gate started to move to the right, and inside a panel hidden in the fence.

Marie drove through it carefully, and then up a long driveway with grass and live oak trees all around. It was almost like driving through the forest, she thought as she made her way up the cement driveway. She arrived at the house and stopped to stare up at it. Three floors of white palace greeted her. At least, it looked like a palace to her. There were six tall columns along the front of the house and rows and rows of windows.

More trees peeked out from each side of the house and she wondered what was in the back. She finished the drive up to the house before she came to a stop in a wide spot on the path. She stared up at the house some more. There were jasmine bushes along the front, and she noted that, despite the heat, none of the windows were open. His power bill must be huge to keep a place that big cool.

She put the car into park, turned it off reluctantly, and opened the door. She wanted to get out. She had been excited about their date ten minutes ago, but now? Now she just felt overwhelmed. This wasn't the kind of place she was supposed to ever be in. Maybe a nice two-story house with a bit of land, and a garage to protect the cars from the summer sunlight, but nothing like this. This was a mansion, and it let you know it.

She started to shut the door, but she remembered how much she'd wanted to spend some time with him alone. She was paying someone to stay with her mother she'd wanted this date so much. A nice dinner, some time alone with him, and maybe a little more than the kisses he'd traced along her wrist was all she wanted. That wasn't too much to ask, was it?

Marie wanted to actually have some private time with him. Before now, there'd always been an audience around them, even if nobody paid attention to them. It was still out in the open, where anyone could see them. The hunger in his eyes had only grown over the long weeks and she'd felt a reciprocation of that hunger in her own body. She wanted him, and for the first time in her life, she wanted to have something of her own. Something that hadn't been tainted by her mother.

Matteo was that thing, that one thing she needed more than anything else right now. He was all she wanted, and if she left right now, she knew she'd never have it. She'd be too much of a coward to face him if she stood him up.

With a deep breath and stiff spine, she got out of the car. She stood as tall as she could in the unfamiliar stilettos, even though her ankles wanted to wobble. With a gentle push, she shut the car door softly and walked up the porch that covered at least three sides of the house. Pride alone gave her the impetus to press the button of the doorbell. She didn't really notice a lot about the house once she was on the porch, though she did see quite a few rocking chairs and tables placed around. Other than that, all she saw was the white front door and the light that shone through narrow panes of glass on each side of the barrier.

"Good evening, Miss Hebert. If you'll follow me," the same bored, male voice greeted her, but this time he was in corporal form. She didn't know if he was a butler, a friend, or a family member, so she just nodded her head and came into the foyer. He was a tall man, in his mid-40s, with a bald head and bored brown eyes. He'd be handsome if he didn't look as though he was about to expire from lack of any kind of emotion other than indifference.

"Thank you," she said and ignored the

man to look around. Dark brown wood comprised two sets of winding stairs, one on each side of the foyer, that likely went up to the second floor. The bored man didn't take her up the stairs, instead, he took her through and into a room that she could only assume was a library because of all of the books on shelves along the walls. There was a couch, two armchairs, and a desk in the room as well.

"Please wait here, miss," the man said before he left the room.

"Of course. Thank you," Marie said quickly, nervous now that she was in the house.

She wrung her hands together and tried to convince herself not to bolt out of the place. His house had a library! Her house had a stack of books that she'd borrowed from the library in town. Maybe she should get back in her car and go to a daiquiri shop, get herself a nice chocolate daiquiri, and head home. This life wasn't for her at all.

But she'd always known that, hadn't she? It wasn't like it was a sudden surprise that Matteo was rich, she'd known that all along, she reminded herself. If he wanted her, despite the implications she'd made that she was poor, then there must be something he liked about her. And if he'd spent a month with a coffee every other day as their only dates, then he was after more than just sex.

Which, if she was honest with herself, she wanted too. She'd dreamed about it every night for weeks now, since the first time his lips brushed over her knuckles. They'd been long, hot dreams that turned her days into long hours of restlessness. The only time she didn't feel that itch of restlessness was when she with Matteo. She smiled as she thought about the fact that she was closer to him than she'd been before. A sudden knock at the closed door made her jump and turn in the armchair to the right of the couch she'd chosen to sit in.

"I told Tommy to bring you something to drink, that awful man." Matteo came in, his cologne already scenting the air as he approached. She loved that cologne, it smelled so delicious, but she had no idea what brand it was. "How are you, Marie?"

He bent down to kiss her cheek and smiled at her. He stood up right away and turned to a drinks cabinet she hadn't noticed.

"I'm fine and I'd like some ginger ale if you have it." She only had a couple of hours so she'd save alcoholic beverages for dinner. She'd have to drive herself home after this, so she wanted to be careful.

"I do, indeed. I got some earlier from the store, just for you." He brought her a glass filled with the golden liquid and ice. "Dinner will be ready in about ten minutes. Do you want to look around outside for a moment?"

"I would love to." She stood up and followed him as well as she could in the unfamiliar heels. She managed to stay upright at least and followed him into a fairy haven in the sparkling twilight. The sunlight had only just started to dim and the lights had only just started to come on, but she could see box hedges cut into curls and lines that turned much of the area into a maze with small gardens of many varieties spread out around them. Just behind that, she saw a large deck and a pool, with a small cabin to the side.

As the clear white LED lights came on, sparkles started to reflect back from the water of the pool, and it turned into a magical place of wonder. Marie breathed in with admiration and smiled when her lungs filled with air that was scented by more jasmine.

"It's beautiful here, Matteo." She couldn't believe how elegant it all was, and how very beautiful it looked. She'd never have guessed this was back here from the front exterior that gave away so little. It was merely a display of wealth, so the garden in the back was really special.

"I'm glad you like it, Marie. Let me show you where the dining room is now." He took her empty left hand and guided her through a maze of hallways to the dining room. It was a large, open room, decorated in white with splashes of dark wood. She'd noted that most of the rooms were white with color added by furnishings or art that decorated each room.

This room had a long, dark table, that was set for only two. Marie counted the chairs as Matteo pulled out a seat for her and then sat down beside her. There were enough chairs to seat 50 people. That was a seriously long table.

She turned to her right to face him and tried to hide how intimidated she was with a cheerful smile. There was so much wealth on display, it overwhelmed her.

"Don't be frightened, my dear. The evening has only just begun, and yes, you deserve to be here as much as I do. Relax, enjoy your meal, and let your cares go, for just a little while.

She couldn't say no to him.

10

Marie was glad she'd asked him for a light dinner when he asked her if she'd ever been swimming in the dark. The sun had set while they ate a dinner of roast chicken and salad. She'd tasted very little of it because she was too keyed up.

He was so close, so warm, but at the same time, he could probably tell she had no idea which fork to use out of the setting before her. She'd watched him and hoped he hadn't noticed her pause. She also didn't know which glass was a water glass and which was for wine. She'd let him pour the beverages just so he wouldn't know.

Now, they were outside, taking in the cool breeze as they watched the water in the pool, and the fireflies dance in the darkness. They were on two Adirondack style loungers, only feet from the water. The clear water looked inviting, lit from below. Far more inviting than the bayou, where anything could swim by or pull you under. Or attach itself to you in the case of leeches.

She shuddered and turned to speak to him. "I have, but only in the bayou. And only once. I was about 8 years old and tired of being hot. I snuck out one night and came home screaming because I was covered in leeches."

"Now that sounds like a good reason to scream," his chuckle was deep and throaty, and amusement made his eyes light up. "You must have been terrified."

"I was! I thought they'd suck all my blood out and I'd die before I even made it back to the house." She laughed with him for a moment, until she remembered how her mother had slapped her and asked her if she'd been out there with boys.

The smile disappeared and she felt how her face fell. She took a deep breath and decided to change the subject instead of dwelling on the past.

"Is that an offer to swim?" she asked and looked at the beautiful blue tile that tinged the water delicately.

"If you'd like." He glanced down at his watch and smiled. "We have an hour and 15 minutes before you have to go."

"It would be nice." She sat up and looked at him, uncertain. She'd never been in a pool that nice, or in a pool with a man at all.

"Then swim you shall, Marie." He stood up, took her hand, and pulled her up to follow him to the small cabin at the end of the pool. Inside, there were three rooms: a private bathroom, a changing room, and the room where all the equipment and supplies for the pool's maintenance were kept.

"There are new swimsuits there, just

basic things, but they're brand new." He pointed at a closet and spoke again. "There are towels in there as well. Take whatever you like."

"Thanks." She looked away, uncertain of how to ask him to leave so she could change.

"I'll leave you to it," he said before she could ask and left her in the room.

She breathed a sigh of relief and opened the cabinet doors. She found a simple black bathing suit in her size and took out a towel. She removed her clothes quickly, and carefully hid her undergarments in her dress. She put those down on a chair and slid into the bathing suit.

It fit her fine, without revealing too much so she put the towel around her waist and left the cabin. Matteo had on a pair of low-slung swimming trunks that went down to his mid-thigh. He was speaking to another tall man, but this one had black hair and scowled in her direction as she came out. The man's face frowned even more as she came to a stop and stared at them.

She had time to take in the beauty of Matteo's back before he turned to see what had made the other man frown so much. Marie was a little scared of that other man, but he left when Matteo made a quick gesture at the man to leave them. She smiled and focused on the man that really counted.

Matteo. She saw his hard chest with pronounced muscles and a tattoo of a crown on the right side. His chest narrowed down to his waist, with abs carved out of stone. He was a muscular man, from his calves and thighs to his biceps, but not in a frightening way. It was more like he'd sculpted each section of his body to perfection and had stopped there.

She went up to him and was glad the swimsuit was cut high. It made her legs look long and lithe. The top of the suit pressed her breasts together and gave her cleavage a boost. All in all, it was an appealing look, and she hoped he liked what he saw.

"Ready? The water is warm, but not too warm." His deep voice soothed away the last of her frazzled nerves as they went into the water together.

She'd learned to swim on her own, so she wasn't an expert at it, but she could remain above the water at least. Somebody gave her mom an above-ground pool one summer and Marie put it together, kept it clean, and spent most of the summer in the water. She'd loved it and could have never dreamed that she'd one day swim in something that looked like it belonged in an Italian villa, tucked away in some village somewhere that normal people could never afford to see.

There were marble statues around the pool and grapevines grew to one side, on an arbor that spanned the same length as the pool. The vines were burdened down with grapes and Marie wondered if the fruits would actually be harvested or left there to rot.

The water swirled around her feet as they walked down the steps into the pool. Despite Matteo's reassurance, she was surprised to find it was warm, but not too warm. Just enough to make it comfortable. She waded further into the water, aware of Matteo the entire time. He dove into the water like a seal kept too long on land. He swam along the bottom for a long time, too long as far as Marie was concerned but came up for air with a splash.

"Are you alright?" he asked when he saw her surprised look.

"Yes, I just didn't know people could hold their breath that long." She'd made it to chest height and started to tread water.

"I was on the swim team in high school. I was also on the swim team for the university I went to in California. I've never quite got over my love of swimming." He smiled and rolled his eyes at himself. She could only laugh because she'd not taken part in any sports while she was in school and hadn't gone to a university.

Instead of answering, she pushed herself under the water and then came right back up. She came back up to find that Matteo had swum very close to her. She looked into his eyes as she swiped water from her face and saw... delight?

"What do you want from life, Marie? Obviously, you'd want your mother to be well, but if you could have more than that, what would you ask for?"

"Help. That's about all. I've taken care of my mother for so long now help would be all I wanted," she answered without thinking, she didn't need to. She'd been drowning for years now, under the burden of taking care of her mother with very little training, and very little help. "Sometimes, I wonder if she'll die because I did something wrong or forgot to give her one of her medications. At other times, I wonder what will happen if the power goes off for more than a week. She has to have oxygen and we have tanks that she can use just in case the power goes off, but it's only a week's supply. There are so many things to worry about, and it would be nice, even if it was just for one week, to not worry about it all on my own."

That might have revealed far more than she had planned to, she worried as she looked up into his face. He wore a solemn expression, one that made his lively eyes sad. Regret tugged at her heart for making him sad, and she turned away, to swim out further into the deeper water.

"Sorry, I didn't mean to, well, ruin the moment," she murmured when she was far enough away from him. She'd had to escape the sadness in those eyes, it felt too much like pity.

"You didn't. You just made me realize that not everyone wants a mansion in the hills and a million dollars to go with it." He went back to the steps and sat down. "You are so different from most of the people I know, Marie."

"That's because I'm not rich." Again,

she'd spoken automatically, and felt her cheeks turn red. "Sorry, that sounded mean."

"No, I suspect you're right actually. I know poor people in New York, people from the projects, from the country too, the more rural areas where you can still find the working poor. But none of them are like you. They'd still want money and a mansion if I asked them that question."

"Mansions require staff and energy to keep them warm and cool. Then there's the furniture that goes inside of them, and everything else. The million dollars wouldn't last long. But then, there are trade-offs. There are the taxes we pay. Take my house for example. It's smaller than yours, much smaller, but I bet I pay more taxes on it than you do on this one."

He nodded as if he understood, and she swam closer to him. She didn't feel so pitied now. His expression now was more curious, maybe even amused.

"You can look to be rich, and still be

poor though. The cost of upkeep on this house would also eat into that million dollars. It wouldn't last long. But a little bit of help, that would do me a whole lot of good. If I didn't have to care for my mom seven days a week, I could maybe go back to school, start the degree I never got to start. I could change both of our lives with a degree, and maybe afford to fix up the house that we live in, too. That makes more sense to me than a giant house and a bunch of money that will disappear before I know it."

"You're right." He leaned forward, his elbows on his knees as he watched her swim. He studied her, her eyes, her lips, what he could see of her torso. "You're an amazing woman, Marie."

"No, just sensible, I'm afraid." She brushed off his compliment, but still smiled at him with pleasure. "I've lived with her my whole life, and it's not always a good thing, but she at least taught me to be sensible."

"What do you mean, it hasn't always

been nice? Isn't she kind to you?" His brows knit together as he asked the question.

"My mother was on the verge of being a film star when she got pregnant with me." She'd avoided talk of her mother when she could help it but now felt like the right time to explain a little more about her life. "She was dating a man she didn't know was married, and there was a car accident. Some men shot at them and my father wrecked the car he was driving. He died, but Mom lived. She was in a coma for months. Too long to..."

"To what, Marie?" he asked, obviously confused.

"To get rid of me." She faced him, her chin up, her shoulders back, a portrait of pride, but the bitterly twisted line of her mouth revealed her emotions. "She was stuck with me, and that ruined her life. It ruined her film career. Life hasn't been easy for her."

It was the mantra she'd repeated her entire life, that her mother had repeated so many times it was ingrained in her psyche. She hadn't been able to get rid of Marie and because of it, Ruby's life had never been the same.

"That's not your fault." His confusion deepened, and she knew he couldn't understand. She barely did but it had been a truth she always knew. Marie ruined Ruby's life, even though it was Ruby's actions that resulted in Marie being born.

Marie continued to tread water, but she couldn't look at him. "What about you? What was your childhood like?"

"Oh, my parents were the usual children of generations of Italians born in America. We did the whole Catholic church thing, and went to private schools..." His words tapered off as he looked away. "They were the usual kind of parents, I guess."

That didn't reveal a whole lot. "Usual" could be anything in the world today. Bad, good, brilliant, lackluster. He hid a lot of things about himself, she'd noticed over the last few weeks. He never frowned or went silent, he just... gave vague answers that could mean anything.

"Are they still alive?" she asked, curious to know so much more. She'd moved closer to him, almost close enough to touch him.

Instead of answering her, he pulled her close and kissed her. She knew it was another distraction technique, but she didn't care. His lips were on hers, and his body, so silky, hard, and warm, was against hers. She shivered as sheer pleasure coursed through her body and her skin went tight. She could feel her nipples, trapped in the swimsuit, pressed against his chest, and somehow it made the kiss even more exciting.

Matteo groaned out his pleasure and pulled her over him so that she was straddling his body. She looked into his eyes, hungry to see the want that was always there.

"I've wanted this for so long now, Marie," his ragged voice tugged at some secret place inside of her that thrilled at that sound.

Her hips moved, pushed her bottom down against the hard length of him, and she gasped. Her eyes went wide with surprised pleasure as she realized he really did want her. Like that!

He kissed her again until every thought in her head had disappeared and all she could think of was how he felt, how he tasted, and the sound of his ragged breathing. But then, he pulled away. He pushed her off his body, gently, and stood up to leave the pool.

"I want you, Marie, but not yet. You have to go. Your mother needs you. We'd better get dressed." He walked away, and she wondered if it was because he knew that if he stayed with her a moment longer, she wouldn't be going home any time soon. Because that's exactly how she felt. Like she'd throw everything away, just for him.

11

Marie stared at the spines of books on row after row of shelves. Nothing caught her eyes. Not the gruesome red font on a black spine, nor the splash of aqua blue against a purple background. The name of one of her favorite authors was ignored, as she traced her fingers down the shelf. Her mind was far, far away.

Well, not that far. Only a few miles away. On Matteo and that pool of his. She'd gone home the night before, certain that the next time she was with him, at his house, that her virginity would disappear. There was some reckless, clanging urge inside of her that said she needed to go back to him, and she'd fought with that urge all night. She'd had to get up twice to change the pads under her mother and clean her up, she couldn't leave her mother alone in that state.

And she wouldn't. Above all, Marie was a good daughter, even if her mother told her she wasn't. She knew she was. She might be sheltered from the rest of the world, but she'd been out in it. At least, into the town. The bad children were the ones that abandoned their parents, that left them to struggle alone. Those were bad children. Marie took care of her mother. She'd given up everything, in fact, to make sure her mother was cared for.

She and Matteo hadn't talked about their parents or their childhoods much. They'd talked about the town, about the people that passed by, about how nice it would be to go out together. She'd told him about her mother, that she was ill, but she hadn't filled in the details. Not until last night anyway, she thought as her fingers stopped on a shelf.

She'd spotted a book she'd been waiting on for months now. It had finally been returned to the shelves, so she picked it up, though she wasn't really interested in it at the moment. She might be later, though, so she pulled it off the dark panel of wood and moved along. The shelves went well over her head, so she was hidden as she neared the end of the row she was in.

"Karen, how good to see you!" a voice said quietly from the row to Marie's right, loud enough for her to hear.

"Lydia, how are you?"

Lydia Metrejean, the town gossip. Marie didn't want to be anywhere near the woman, so she stopped and hoped they would move along soon.

"Oh, I'm fine Karen. I hear there's a new man in town." Lydia's voice almost shook with the excitement of a new piece of gossip.

"You mean that Mafia guy? I think his name's Matthew," Karen said softly, just as pleased to pass on information as Lydia was.

"I think it's Matteo," Lydia said smugly before she carried on. "I heard he was super rich and very handsome."

"I saw him at the café with that Marie Hebert. I always knew she'd end up getting into some kind of trouble." Karen's previously happy tone now dripped with venom. "Her mother was trouble and she will be too. She'll end up the same way if she keeps hanging out with that guy."

"Oh, that's really too bad. He's damaged goods now. I wouldn't touch anything that came into contact with Marie Hebert."

Marie couldn't help but frown, but she stayed put. She didn't want either of the two harpies to know she had heard them.

"So, what's this about Mafia ties? Is he bringing in drugs or something?" Karen prompted.

"I heard it's gambling more than drugs."

"Well, we like our gambling down here, don't we?" Karen snorted and must have realized the time because she quickly said she had to go. "I have to pick up Bryanny from school. I'll see you soon, Lydia. Stay away from crime bosses!"

Lydia chuckled as her friend left, but Marie frowned even more. Crime boss? She knew he was rich, that was blatantly obvious, but a crime boss? Mafia even?

Her mother's warning her whole life came back to her now. Stay away from Mafia men, Ruby had warned. Marie had always rolled her eyes at her mother's warnings. Not because it wasn't good advice, but because of where they lived. How would she ever come near a man in the Mafia stuck out here in the back of nowhere? Yet, Lydia and Karen had both said that Matteo was in the Mafia, or was some kind of crime boss, at least.

Marie thought it over as she hid from Lydia. When the other woman went to the front of the one-story library, Marie moved deeper into the rows of books until she was hidden well in the back. If Matteo was in the Mafia, did it change how she felt about him?

She didn't know what love was, but she knew he made her heart race and her stomach turn into a knot every time she thought about him or went near him. Was that love? And if so, did the news that he might be in a criminal organization change that?

She leaned back against the wall and closed her eyes.

A smile spread over her face. The news changed her thoughts about him, but rather than scare her, it thrilled her. She'd been a good girl her entire life, and it got her nowhere. She was an outcast in the town, her own mother hated her, and the only friend she had was a woman that was paid by the state to care for her mother. Being good brought fuck all to her life.

Matteo, on the other hand, had brought passion, love, pleasure. He brought her promises that she knew he'd die to keep, even if he hadn't made those proclamations. She knew him to be a man's man, maybe even a little old-fashioned in his ideas on gender roles. She knew that from the way he held out her chair for her when she'd come into the café, and how he would order for them both.

Matteo was also a man of his word. If he said he would be somewhere, he was there. If he promised her something, he did whatever it took to make it happen. He might not be a saint, that smug smirk of his told her he was well-convinced of his own abilities in many fields, but he was... honest.

That might not be the right word, she decided, if he was involved in criminal activities. Whatever the right word was, she didn't care, she finally decided. He was good to her, he wanted her, and she wanted him. She wasn't a saint either, she just didn't have a choice about whether to be good or not. Her own sense of what was right and wrong made her stay with her mother, despite the abuse she'd taken from the woman.

He'd given her a new phone the third week they knew each other. They often exchanged texts and she called him when her mother was asleep. Every day he'd send at least two texts, one to say good morning and one to say goodnight. No matter what, she got those texts every day, and it made her feel special for the first time in her life.

That probably should have her worried, but Marie wasn't. Matteo had given her far more than a phone. He'd given her hope. She knew she had a purpose, a reason to live, her mother needed her, but he gave her hope that there was so much more than that.

She picked up a couple of more books on the new release stand and went to check out. She didn't know which books she'd picked exactly, but she wasn't worried. In the boring hours of the day, she'd read anything to pass the time.

"Is that all, Marie?" the pretty librarian

asked with an awkward smile. Her name tag said Jennifer, and she had light brown hair and pretty blue eyes. She was new to the town, so she'd been nice to Marie at first. Today, however, a strange tightness had shown up around her eyes when Marie walked into the building. Marie knew someone had whispered vile things to the young woman. Things that were probably true if they were about her mother.

Fuck, Marie thought. Now even the librarian cringed at the sight of her. That was just… perfect.

"Yes, Jennifer. Thanks." Marie handed over her library card and got out of the building as quickly as she could. She didn't want the young woman to see the way her hands shook and how much she was fighting back tears.

"I hate this place," she said out loud, even though she didn't mean to. "I hate this place, and the people, and most of all, I hate the fact that my mother made me a pariah in this awful town!"

These were things she wanted to talk to someone about, anyone if it meant she could just get it all out. She'd considered going to see a counselor, but she didn't think she was necessarily depressed or anything. She just felt… trapped. She always had been, until Matteo came along, that is.

She drove home with the memory of his breath on her skin, the way his fingers had slid down her neck, how it felt to press down into him to tantalize her. If her mother was asleep, she'd text him, she decided. Or maybe she'd call him.

She thought about the tattoos she'd seen on him. She liked them, liked the rebellion that had spurred him into getting the ink. He wasn't exactly like the bikers she'd known in the town. They all seemed, sort of, well, dirty to her. Matteo was clean, right down to his perfect fingernails.

He was dangerous, he could break her heart, or he could break her, and that didn't frighten her at all; in fact, it excited her. That was living: taking risks, hoping for the best, and waiting to see what came of the chance taken. That was the kind of life she wanted. She wanted intrigue, romance, and *passion*.

She was tired of being good. She was tired of always being safe. For once in her life, she wanted to know what it felt like to be more than just alive.

She turned the car off and walked into the house. There was a smell. That smell. She rolled her eyes into her head, but it wasn't frustration. It was reality setting in. This would be her life until her mother's illness came to an end. And there was only one way that would happen.

"Hi, Marie. Don't worry about this. I have a few minutes, so I'll clean her up. Get settled in and I'll see you in the kitchen." Jane's face was red, despite the air conditioner her friend had been kind enough to donate to them. Marie was sympathetic, she knew it wasn't just the heat that caused that redness. It had more to do with trying not to breathe too deep until the mess was cleaned up.

Marie simply nodded her head and waited for Jane.

"She's more lively today, but I think she'll sleep tonight, for a change." Jane sighed as she came into the room and washed her hands at the stainless-steel kitchen sink. She'd washed them in the bathroom but, like Marie, she washed them in the kitchen too, just to be sure. Hygiene was key to keeping down contamination and infection, for all of them.

Marie looked down at her hands, raw and a little red from all the washing she did. She used hand cream on them, but that only helped a little. Sometimes she would massage cooking oil into them, just to try and help the dryness she would end up with. That worked when it was really bad.

"Oh, here, I brought you this. It really helps your hands." Jane winked at Marie and handed her a white tube. It was some kind of specialty hand cream for those with work-roughened hands.

"Thanks!" she said with a grateful smile. From the label, Marie knew she'd never be able to afford a tube of hand cream like that. She squeezed a dab out into her hands and saw it was more an ointment than a cream. "That's different."

"It is. It's what I use, and well, I think you want to look your best, lately, don't you?"

Marie went still and she looked at the nurse with a quizzical gaze. "Maybe."

She laughed after she spoke. She hadn't exactly told Jane about Matteo, but Jane knew she'd been seeing someone. As the whole town apparently knew she'd been seen talking to Matteo, it was likely Jane had been told too. Or asked. Most people knew Jane was Ruby's home health nurse.

"Just enjoy yourself, Marie. Don't get to, um serious." A flush ran down Jane's face, deep down into the top of her pink uniform top, and she looked down at the floor. "But

I hope you get some happiness, honey. You deserve it."

"Thanks, Jane." Marie wanted to hug her but wasn't sure she should, suddenly.

She wasn't sure why, Jane had always been open to affection from Marie, but now, well, she felt a little distance there that hadn't been there before. Marie knew it was something in herself that put that wall up, maybe the idea that she was really a grown-up?

In the end, Jane took Marie in her arms and hugged her tightly. "Just have fun, honey, remember that, alright?"

"I will, Jane. Thank you." Whatever the problem was disappeared the moment Marie was wrapped in Jane's arms. She sank into the embrace and smelled the other woman's perfume. This was what having a mom was supposed to have been like, she thought. But her mother wasn't that kind, she reminded herself and pulled away. "I hope you have a good day, Jane."

"I will, honey. One way or another. Use

that ointment in the morning and before you go to bed. It works. See you tomorrow."

Jane left finally and Marie took a deep breath. She walked back to her mother's room and saw she was asleep. Even in her sleep, she looked bitter, Marie noted. She wasn't sure if that was from pain or if her mother had always looked like that when she was asleep.

She wanted to be able to tell her mother about Matteo, to tell her the gossip she'd heard, but she knew that Ruby would just end up having a fit. Any hint that he was Mafia would send Ruby over the edge. It was better, then, to keep the news to herself. To protect her new relationship from her mother's taint. It hurt Marie to think like that, but she knew it was the truth. Ruby corrupted things, it was just who she was.

12

"You can just take that shit and shove it up your ass, Marie. I'm sick of that mushy crap. I want a steak!" Ruby threw the bowl of oatmeal at Marie and barely missed her head. The plastic bowl hit the wall and slid slowly down the wall, the oatmeal adding friction to hold it in place.

"Mom," Marie said, her patience with her mother almost gone for the day. She'd dealt with her all day long. Jane had called to say she was ill with pneumonia and wouldn't be there that day. Marie was sympathetic to the other woman and her illness, but her patience with her mother was worn thin.

A new nurse would come tomorrow, but for today, Marie was all her mother had, and she was showing her ass already. The day would end in tears, Marie knew it.

"What? I'm the grown-up here, I tell you what I want. Now, get in that kitchen and cook me a steak, you lazy bitch." Ruby glared at Marie as if she could get up and slap her daughter if she wanted to, she just didn't want to make that effort.

Marie knew better. Ruby couldn't get out of that bed on her own if the house caught on fire, much less to slap Marie.

"I'm sorry to tell you, Mom, but I've been an adult for 8 years now. We're both grown now." Marie glared back at her mother; irritation steeled her backbone enough to let her maintain the hard stare. "I'm not making you a steak because you can't swallow it. You are aware of that. I wouldn't withhold food from you, but I'm not going to make another bowl of oatmeal until you tell me you'll eat it."

"I won't! I'm sick of that shit. Call the doctor, I demand you call the doctor." Ruby shook with rage as she screeched at Marie. "If you don't call that charlatan, I'll have Jane call social services on you tomorrow. You can't make me eat that slop anymore!"

Marie sighed and left the room. She came back with a roll of paper towels to clean up the oatmeal. She reminded herself, for the thousandth time, that it was time to pull the carpet up in there. It was clean, but even the dark green color had started to show stains and signs of wear. She couldn't afford a new carpet, so she'd have to just polish the hardwood beneath the carpet.

"Marie! Marie, where's my oatmeal? I'm starving!" Ruby shouted, her voice a totally different tone now. It was confused, maybe even a little frightened.

"It's here on the floor, Mom. Where you threw it, remember?" Marie had to struggle to keep her irritation under control.

"What? I didn't do that! Why do you lie about me so much, Marie?" Ruby promptly burst into tears, and Marie stood up, stunned into silence.

"Pardon?" Marie watched as her mother pressed her face into her hands and cried as if she was heartbroken. This was new.

Marie wasn't a callous person; the sight of her mother's tears didn't leave her completely unmoved. Ruby had been, would always be, an actress and had used more than one tactic to get her way out of her daughter over the years. Marie couldn't help but wonder if this was real or if Ruby really couldn't remember what had just happened.

"I'll get you another bowl, Mom, don't worry." She finished her task and went back to the kitchen for more oatmeal. She heated up a new bowl of the concoction and prepared it how her mother liked it: milk, butter, a little bit of sugar. She took the bowl in and watched as her mother ate the meal as if it was the best thing she'd ever had.

"This is so good, Marie. Thank you." Her mother sniffled as she spoke and wiped at her nose with a tissue. Luckily, Ruby could still use one hand when she was herself, so Marie left the room to clean up the dishes.

Just as she put the last dish in the drainer, she heard a knock at the door. The only visitor they normally had was Jane. Her heart started to trip, and shame washed over her. Matteo hadn't decided to visit her, had he? She didn't want him to see where she lived.

The house needed a new coat of paint, the lawn hadn't been cut in weeks because the mower had died and she hadn't been able to replace it yet, and the place looked like it was falling in. It was structurally sound, the roof didn't leak, but it still looked… unloved.

No, it couldn't be him. She'd texted him to tell him she would be busy and not able to meet him today. He always respected her when she told him she couldn't, or wouldn't, be able to do something. He treated her like a lady. He wouldn't be rude and just show up.

Marie scrunched her hair up into a bun and smoothed her clothes down. If it was him, she didn't want to look a complete mess. Even if she was.

She opened the door to find an unfamiliar woman in her late 40s on the doorstep. "Hi, can I help you? Are you lost?"

"No, I'm sorry, I knocked at the front door, but nobody answered so I came to the backdoor. My name is Regina Murphy. I'm with Bayou State Home Health. I was sent to stay with Ruby Hebert?"

"I'm sorry, who sent you?" Marie frowned and leaned against the doorframe to block any entry, even though the other woman was much taller and rounder than she was.

"I was told to give you this, along with the company's information and my credentials." The woman dug a folder out of what looked like a laptop bag and handed it over to Marie. It was similar to the folder Jane had brought when she first came.

A paperclip held a card that was familiar to Marie and she closed her eyes in disbelief. Matteo had hired a nurse to come to stay with her mother?

"Matteo's paying for this?" she asked the woman, who shrugged.

"I don't know a lot about that, I was just told to give you the file and the card. My company pays me, and they bill the person that arranged for me to come." Regina paused as if she understood the quandary Marie found herself in. "It happens like this sometimes. If you want to call him, that's fine, I understand."

"No, I'm sorry, please come in and join me at the kitchen table. Would you like a glass of iced tea?"

"I don't drink it, but a glass of water would be nice." Regina sat down, put her bag down, and looked around. She didn't look as if she was judging, just familiarizing herself with the place.

Marie got the water and then sat down to go over the papers in the folder. Regina's credentials were there, showing she was more than qualified to care for her mother, as well as a copy of the paid bill for a year of care. Marie's eyes went big as she looked at the sum Matteo had already paid.

"Fuck." She whispered the word so the other woman wouldn't hear.

"Pardon?" Regina sat forward now, her red hair in a ponytail was so long it slid over her shoulder. Green eyes watched Marie.

"Nothing, I just can't believe he's done this. I mean, I know he has, the proof is here." She pointed at the bill. "I just can't believe he's done it. And you don't know anything about who I'm talking about. Sorry. I see you're supposed to work from 8 pm to 8 am?"

"Yes, it's a shift I prefer. Our older patients can have such a hard time at night, I like being there to reassure them and help them to rest."

"You understand my mother also has dementia on top of Parkinson's disease?"

"I do. I'm sorry, I know this is a very unusual way of doing this. We gathered from the man that paid that this wouldn't be the normal situation. I've spent the last 15 years taking care of elderly patients with a variety of health problems. I'm prepared for most things. Even the patients that can't help but act violently. I assure you I've seen it all."

Something about the woman's tone told Marie that the nurse would be perfect for her mother. Regina would do her job and keep the situation under control without panic. Marie glanced back over her credentials again and knew Regina was the perfect fit. She hoped.

"Would you like to meet her?" Marie wasn't even sure it was legal for Matteo to hire a nurse like this, but money talked all over the world and opened doors.

There was a calm air about Regina, and she handled the introduction with Ruby competently. Ruby didn't seem too upset and understood that she would have a new nurse in the evenings. Which meant... oh goodness.

It finally hit Marie exactly what all of this meant. She would have 12 hours free every five days! She could escape, for a little while.

Before she completely collapsed from relief, Marie showed Regina the medicines her mother would have to take, and the ones prescribed to keep her calm if she became too violent. The other woman was familiar with the machines and the precautions she would have to take to keep Ruby comfortable. Marie also showed her where the supplies she might need were kept, and spent time introducing her to the parts of the house she would use.

"I'm sorry, are you allowed to sleep while you do this?" Marie wasn't sure how it worked, so she asked. She'd have prepared a room for the woman if that was the case.

"No, but I'm a night person, so it's fine. I

knit a lot, usually. It just depends on how much your mother sleeps."

"Okay. Well, my number is on the fridge." It was the number to the phone Matteo had given her, so she didn't have to use the minutes on the phone her mother had been given. "I guess, well, I'm going to take a shower, and then, I don't know. I've not had a night off since I was 18."

"Seriously?" Regina asked, then flushed. "Sorry, it's none of my business."

"No, it's fine. We're alone, Mom and I, and I'm paid to take care of her during the day, but not at night. She gets disability, but most of that pays for her medicines and some of the bills. My paycheck pays for what little I can afford from that. A night nurse hasn't been in the cards. This is just, wow, it's just a relief." Marie knew she was rambling, so she smiled and took a deep breath. "I'm going to shower."

"You go on out and enjoy yourself, Marie. It sounds like you deserve a long night out." Regina gave Marie a reassuring smile and nodded with respect. "I'll be here if you get worried, just give us a call."

"I will. Thank you so much!" Marie almost kissed the woman she was so happy but held herself back.

She showered quickly, changed into another old but still wearable dress, this one in black, something she'd sewn herself, and was almost out the door when her mother called her name.

"Marie? Marie! Who's paying for this woman to stay here with me!" Marie cringed at the hateful sound of her mother's voice.

She walked back to the bedroom and looked in at her mother. "I applied for a grant for you Mom, and it was approved. Didn't I tell you? It must have slipped my mind."

Marie kept her face bland, and when she glanced at Regina, she saw the woman nod subtly. She got it, thank goodness. Her mother didn't need to know where the money came from.

"Well, don't you be out whoring around. I'm not raising no babies!" Ruby all but stared a hole into Marie, but Marie stood tall and did her best not to give anything away.

She was about to walk out and do everything her mother had told her not to do. She was going to meet a man that was, supposedly, in the Mafia. She was going to have sex with him if he wanted to, and by heck, she was going to sleep beside him, if he let her. She wanted to sleep peacefully, without interruption, wrapped in the safety of his arms.

That was all she wanted right now, even more than the sex, she just wanted a night without waking up to her mother screeching at her.

"Thank you, Regina. I won't be far. But don't wait up." The nurse had come to stand beside Marie and so Marie whispered to her.

"Enjoy your evening, Marie. However, you choose to do it. I'm not here to judge, at all," Regina whispered back and gave Marie a wink with twinkling green eyes.

Marie smothered a giggle and made to leave the house. She picked up her handbag, slid her phone into it, and got the car keys from the hook. It was time to live.

Matteo had paid a small fortune for her mother's new nurse, and though she knew she should refuse it and tell him to get his money back, she couldn't do it. He'd done this for her. And maybe himself a little too, she thought as she drove to his house.

She'd sent a text that she was on her way, but he hadn't answered it yet. Maybe he was preparing for her, having a shower and all that stuff men did to prepare for a date? Though, she wasn't exactly sure what that was.

She slowed when she saw a small deer bounce across the road, and let it pass before she carried on. He wanted to see her, to spend time with her, and the only way to do that was to make sure someone could stay with Ruby at night. He'd done them both a favor then.

Which was another reason she would agree to this. Even though it was a done deal, she still could have refused, but she didn't. As his house came into view, her heart began to thud in her chest and her palms went moist on the steering wheel. She was about to get everything she wanted. Almost. She'd have to go home early, but tonight? Tonight was hers. If all she had with him was the darkness, then so be it. She'd take it, she thought as she parked and got out of the car. As long as she got to be with him.

13

When she arrived at Matteo's house, Marie took a deep breath, and then knocked on the door. Matteo himself answered this time, and Marie was glad for that. The other guy, the butler or whatever he was, made her nervous with his baleful stare. His gaze said she wasn't good enough, but it wasn't really any of his business was it?

She was in a really good mood for the first time in a really long time, and she showed it when she leaned up to him and placed a kiss on his cheek. He wasn't usually the one that took the kisses. His warm brown eyes radiated pleasure as he took her hand to guide her into the house.

"I thought we'd do something normal people do and watch movies." He held his hand up when she started to speak and laughed. "I know it sounds boring, but how else will we get to know each other better? You can judge a lot about a person from the movies they like."

"That's just it, though. I haven't had time to watch movies in years unless they're on television as I fall asleep. I don't know what I like." She felt awkward now and wanted to change the subject. "And thank you, I know this is for you too, but I really can't thank you enough for hiring that nurse. It's the most generous thing anyone has ever done for me. Oh, and about Regina? She's wonderful, from what I can see."

"It was my pleasure, Marie. And yes, it was for me too, so not completely altruistic of me, was it?" His rueful smile only worked to make her heart melt a little more.

"I suppose not." They walked into a

living room with a black velvet couch that wrapped around a corner of the room to take up two walls. There was a small table at one end, and a large coffee table of dark cherry wood in the middle. An array of remote controls rested on the table and Matteo picked one up.

A large, flat television came on and Marie blinked. She hadn't even seen the appliance until it lit up. It was high on the wall with a video of a lit fireplace going. She'd glanced over it, but now realized it was too high on the wall to be a real fireplace. She blushed when she saw what a stupid mistake she'd made, but Matteo was facing the television, thankfully.

"Alright, I've got this set up to show you all the movies we can watch. You choose by category like this, then you can flip through the movies that are listed." He showed her which buttons to use, and she took the remote. "I'm going to get some drinks and such, I'll be right back."

Marie was almost overwhelmed by the

number of movies she now had access to. She wished she'd worn something else now, maybe sweatpants and a t-shirt would have been more appropriate for this kind of date. She kicked her shoes off, tucked her legs up under her bottom, and scrolled over to a movie that looked interesting from the picture.

"What have you chosen, my dear, or are you still looking?" Matteo called out to her as he pushed a shiny metal trolley into the room. The scent of buttered popcorn, hot-dogs, and quite a few other things filled the air.

"What's all this?" she asked with a de-lighted laugh.

"It's what you can usually get at a the-ater. I hate theaters, personally, but love the food you can get at them. I don't indulge in junk food often, but when I do, I want the good stuff." He gave a dramatic wave at the shelves on the trolley and she laughed again.

Chips, dip, nachos with nacho cheese,

hotdogs with every kind of topping imaginable, candy, cakes, brownies, and quite a few other things waiting to be decadently consumed. Her eyes locked on the melted nacho cheese and the nachos, and she looked up at him. "I'd like those first, please."

"I had a feeling you might." He stacked warm nachos into a bowl and handed her a cup of the melted cheese. "And to drink?"

She saw beer, white wine, and juice. "I'll have the white wine, please."

"Good choice." The glass became frosted as he poured a little of the wine into it, and she took it. The wine was crisp and fruity, a nice taste to go with her snack.

"I like that." She saw he put the bottle back into a bucket of ice and was glad it would stay cold. She did like that taste. What she liked even more was the feeling it gave her. "Right, so I've chosen this movie."

"A thriller. Good choice." He nodded, filled a bowl with popcorn, grabbed a cup of nacho cheese, and sat down with her. He also had a hotdog with chili and coleslaw on it. She decided she might have one of those next, it smelled so good.

She put the movie on, and the lights dimmed down. She looked over to see he had another remote control. "Thrillers are best in the dark."

"I think so too," she smirked at him and leaned over to nudge him. "Thank you."

He turned his face, kissed her forehead tenderly, and winked at her. "Don't mention it."

The movie was over an hour long, and they managed to get through quite a few of the treats on the trolley before it was over. She excused herself after the first movie and went to the bathroom. It was nice to be with him, she thought when she finished and washed her hands. She checked her face and hair, and realized, it didn't matter. They were watching movies in the dark.

When she made it back in, she saw he had an old British comedy movie on the screen, ready to go. She hadn't heard of the men that made it, but he said it was funny, so she gave it a chance. This time, she leaned into him where he rested against the arm of the couch. Her back was pressed into the couch, and her head rested against his right shoulder. His arm went around her easily, as it was something he did often.

She was aware of nothing but his body for the first ten minutes, of the flat plane of his stomach where her hand rested over his white t-shirt. His jean-covered thigh pressed into hers, and his face was just there, above hers. All she'd have to do was look up, and he could kiss her. This was nice though, the simple act of watching a movie together was really nice. It felt... normal.

And normal wasn't something she experienced often. Some greedy little part of her wanted to make this moment last forever. She clasped her arm around him a little tighter and settled in. She could hear his heartbeat, and for a moment, she forgot to pay attention to the movie. She listened to that strong thud.

The sound filled her head, strong and steady, over and over. It was a healthy sound that told her he was alive and happy she was here. When her hand clenched over his stomach involuntarily, his heartbeat picked up but soon calmed down. He was just as aware of her as she was of him that sound told her. Her eyes had closed, but she wasn't aware of it, and she drifted off.

She'd been tired when the new nurse showed up, but with a full belly, and so much comfort around her, against her, she just... drifted.

"I'm going to take you up to my bed, Marie. Is that alright with you?" He'd moved and picked her up before she could even make a sound.

"What? We're watching a movie, aren't we?" She was confused but didn't protest. Instead, she wrapped her arms around his neck and let her head settle against his shoulder.

"It's over, sweetheart. You're tired and need some rest." Matteo moved up the stairs without even breaking a sweat, despite her weight in his arms. He moved down a long hallway, all the way to the end, where an open door waited.

He carried her to the bed, then turned a bedside lamp on. "I bought you a nightgown and some pajamas, I wasn't sure which you'd prefer. Or if you'd want to stay the night, but just in case..."

He let his words trail off and she knew he'd said a lot more than he'd spoken. She could still leave if she wanted to, his words told her, or she could stay. Anything that happened was purely up to her.

"I'll take the nightgown, please." She might have been dead to the world five minutes ago, but she was fully awake now. She was in his bedroom, his private domain.

It was a small room, but still larger than her own bedroom. There was a large oak dresser towards one side of the room, a closet with two doors, a floor mirror, and the four-poster bed that she now sat on. It was covered with an emerald green fleece blanket that was the softest thing she'd ever felt and dark green sheets. Two pillows on each side made a fluffy backrest as he brought the nightgown to her.

She'd thought maybe he would buy her a sexy nightgown, something exotic, but more than likely uncomfortable. Instead, he bought a cotton gown, with an empire waist. It was soft, comfortable, yet somehow sensual, even though it was virginal white. She liked it and thanked him for it.

"There's a screen just there, that you can change behind if you want." He pointed into a dark corner and she saw the screen there.

She took the gown, thanked him again, and went to change behind the black silk screen. She took off everything she had on and put on the nightgown. The straps were adjustable, so she fiddled with them until they supported her breasts perfectly. She had no idea what she looked like, but she didn't care.

She was nervous, she'd never slept in a man's bed before, or with a man or anything else with a man. This was all new to her, and she didn't know the rules, but Matteo didn't seem to notice, or mind, her lack of knowledge. With one last deep breath, she left the screen and found Matteo in the bed.

He had on a pair of black pajama bottoms and a black tank top. The impression was sensual, far more than she thought men could be. He looked at her with a faint smile on his face, and her heart skipped a beat. She was really about to do this. With a faint smile of her own, she got into the bed and pulled the covers over her body.

"Everything alright?" he asked and turned to face her.

"Fine, thank you. I've just, never done this." She looked down at her hands nervously. "It's all new to me."

"Don't worry, Marie. You're safe with

me." He took her hands and held them in his. "I'm not going to do anything you don't want me to do. Now, slide down next to me. I want to look at you. I've spent far too many nights dreaming about this."

Her breath caught in her chest at his admission, but she did as instructed. Her heart began to race as she felt his hard body next to hers, so solid and soothing, but so nerve-wracking at the same time. She wanted to touch him, to throw herself over him and touch and kiss every part of him, but she was too afraid to move. What if she did something wrong? What if she hurt him, or did something she shouldn't?

So, she let him guide her. Softly, he placed his hand against her hip. She started to breathe heavier, her eyes glued to his face. He looked curious, but not aggressive or disgusted. That was a good thing. She started to relax, and her breath evened out. His hand moved just a little, over her hip where it narrowed in the middle, and then up, over the outline of her ribs.

Desire flared within her as her nerves came to life. He was so close to her breast he'd only have to move his fingers... up... and he would cup the weight in his hand. Her nipples went tight, her toes curled, and she bit her bottom lip between her teeth to keep quiet. Just a little, Matteo, please move your hand just a little more, she thought to herself.

It didn't occur to her to ask him, he was the one that knew how this worked, he was the boss, for now. She'd let him show her how to do this right.

She nearly groaned in frustration when his hand moved down her hip again, but his lips prevented it. His face came down to hers and she tasted his tongue against hers. Her eyes closed as the taste of mint exploded on her tongue and his scent filled her nose. His hand moved down, in a direction she hadn't yet thought about.

Over the cotton pooled at her hips, his hand slid down further, to the place between her legs. She moaned up into his mouth, her hands now around his head to hold his mouth against hers. Something hot, red, and consuming took her over and she breathed heavily through her nose. Her hips jerked when his fingers flattened the cotton of her nightgown over her mound, and she cried out with shocked pleasure when he found something, *something,* between her legs that felt oh so fucking good.

He broke away from her kiss, at the same time something hard pressed into her hip, and she knew it was him, the evidence of how excited he was. She wasn't totally innocent, after all, she had taken health class, and read a lot of books that involved sex. She'd just never had it.

"If you think this feels good, Marie, let me show you something even more spectacular," Matteo whispered against her ear, hot breath against hot skin. His fingers moved, bunched the cotton at the bottom of her gently rounded stomach before they slid down again. Smoothly, along the silky skin of her body, his fingers moved. The sensation of his skin down there made her mind go blank. When the digits slid into her folds, found her slick and hot, colors began to flit into her mind, but she didn't notice. All she knew was how it felt to have his fingers there.

When he found that spot again, captured it between his two fingers and *tugged*, she made a noise she knew must be obscene, but she couldn't help it. It was guttural, harsh, and not at all feminine, or so she thought. The way he pressed his hips into her told her differently. He liked that sound that movement said. He wanted more of those sounds.

That's when she stopped holding back, when she let herself go completely. Because if this felt that damn good, the rest of it must be more than she could comprehend. She wanted this, but she wanted the rest too. She wanted whatever that aching pleasure he now strummed to life within seemed to be driving her towards.

"Matteo," she whispered his name on

dry lips, her hands kneading the muscles of his shoulders.

"Soon, Marie, just feel for now, baby." He moved again, this time to rest his head against the flat of her stomach. She heard him inhale and knew he must be inhaling her. Images, wants, needs, filled her head, as his head moved lower, as if he couldn't resist that one little taste he wanted.

Marie let her head fall back, waited, breath held, as his lips moved lower, over her, into her. Her hands found his head, dug into his silky hair, and pulled as his tongue came out and *licked* her. It was anticipated, that sensation, but Marie had no idea how truly good it would feel, not until he did it, and when she groaned this time, she groaned his name.

He moved, then settled between her legs and opened her to him with his hands. One on each side of her folds, revealed all she had to give him. She knew she should probably worry about... something... but she couldn't. All she could do was wait, want, need for him to continue. He looked his fill of her before he moved again, on his knees, to taste her all over again.

A strangled sound of need was muffled when he sucked her between his lips. A finger teased at her opening but did not enter her. She wanted him to, wanted to know what it would feel like to have a man penetrate her, but he held back. Her groan of frustration didn't earn her anything but a harder tug of his lips on that area that felt so good.

She knew what it was called, but she'd never said the word out loud, had never meant to. She knew all the words, but she'd never thought she'd have a chance to say them, much less use those parts. Now, he had her flat on her back, knees up, hands clenched in his hair, as he used his mouth to make her...

"Fuck! Matteo!" She strangled the words out as something exploded, something down there, that pulsed straight up her body and into her brain. She felt muscles contort, and her body quaked as time after time, ecstasy wracked through her every nerve and cell.

He didn't say a word, he was too busy to break the contact. And she was glad because she didn't want this feeling to ever end.

14

When she couldn't take anymore, when the sensation became too much, she pushed at his head. Matteo swiftly moved his head away, but he didn't leave the position he was in. She floated in some peaceful place where nothing existed but him and her.

She could feel his hot skin against hers, could feel the slight sheen of sweat on her skin. She heard the sound of his harsh breathing and knew he was just as excited as she was. Their breath slowed together, and when she could open her eyes again, she looked down.

"It's not over, is it?" She knew the question revealed the truth to him when she saw his left eyebrow arch a little. She was a virgin, but she'd never said as much to him. Not until now, when her stupid question gave it away. He looked pleased, though, so she didn't look away.

"It is for tonight, Marie. There's no need to rush anything." He moved her legs off of his shoulders and came up to rest on the pillow beside hers. "You're different, do you understand? You're sweet and kind, and so in need of love. You deserve to enjoy every moment that we have together, Marie, and I'm going to make sure of that."

She felt torn now. That one phrase, so in need of love, had stung a little, but the rest? The rest was more than she knew she could hope for. She saw relationships come and go in this town, sometimes in a matter of days. People didn't seem to want anything more than a moment of pleasure now before they went back to their cell phone or laptop. She needed to be loved, she knew that, and he'd said she deserved it. In the end, glee won out, and she smiled at him, happier than she'd ever been in her life. Even the moment when she opened the letter that said she'd been accepted to LSU hadn't been this good.

"Thank you, Matteo." She put her hand against his cheek and wished her nails were manicured, but then she saw his eyes and forgot to care. They were kind eyes, eyes of a man that would give her the world if he could. Did he love her?

It didn't really matter to her right now. Love was something she didn't know how to define anyway, not with her upbringing. She knew it was supposed to be something about undying devotion and lots of sex, and having babies, but what were the real emotions involved? She had no idea, and the maelstrom of emotions inside of her right now didn't help.

"Get some rest, Marie, and just relax, baby. That's all you have to do." He tucked her under his arm, with her head against his chest. She listened to the sound of his heart, the whisper of every breath he took, and before she knew it, she was asleep.

Her dreams were filled with him, with the things she wanted to explore with him. They were fantasies of possibilities, and her mind drew solely on instinct to flesh the scenes out. It didn't really matter what they did, the focus was purely on pleasure, hours and hours of it. The things they could do, the moments they could have, the places they could do those things in.

When she opened her eyes, the sun was just coming up. Her body was sore and a few places throbbed, but she didn't mind. She stretched under the blanket, the cold air-conditioned climate a luxury she had never experienced before. She knew it was part of the reason she'd slept so well. The other reason was still warm and asleep beside her.

She slid out of the bed and made her way out of the room. She found a bathroom behind the door just down from Matteo's bedroom. She did her business, took a shower, and slipped back into his room to dress. When she finished, she went to the side of the bed and kissed him softly on the cheek.

He jerked awake his eyes wide on hers. "Oh, it's you." He smiled and cleared his throat as he pushed his torso off the bed. "Is it time for you to go?"

"It is. I have to get home to Mom now, and let the nurse go." She brushed the hair out of his face and kissed his forehead. "Thank you. Text me later, when you're awake again, okay?"

"You know it, baby. Be careful driving home." His hands lingered on her cheek but then fell away as sleep took him again.

Marie's smile was happy as she left the bedroom. It was still in place when she retrieved her shoes from the living room. And when she got in the car. It was only as she started the car up and drove away that the smile began to dim on her face.

When her house came into view, the

smile disappeared completely. She hated the way she dreaded walking into the house, but she had to. She pulled in, stopped the car, and got out. The nurse met her at the door and Marie's smile returned at last.

"Sleep well?" the woman asked with a cheerful gleam in her eye.

"I did actually," Marie answered, and wondered why. She felt some kind of kinship with this woman. Maybe it was something that came with caretakers of the elderly and disabled. You bonded more quickly, maybe? Or maybe it was just that the woman knew what life was like outside of work and was happy that Marie had finally got to experience it too. It didn't really matter, either way, she knew the woman was pleased for her. "How was she, Regina?"

"She was fine, really. She watched TV until around midnight, then she went to sleep. She's still asleep now." Regina was tall, a little on the chubby side, but it suited her frame. She was pretty, Marie thought, but she could tell the woman would be tough when she needed to be.

"Are you kidding me?" Her mother hadn't slept through an entire night in years. Marie sat down at the kitchen table and Regina went to the coffee pot. She held it up and Marie nodded. Regina poured them both coffee and sat down at the table. A tray in the middle of the table held coffee creamer and sugar, but Marie only used creamer.

"She asked for her sleeping pill at around 11, so I gave her that, and she's slept ever since." Regina held up part of a blanket she'd been knitting. "This didn't exist when you left earlier if that tells you anything."

"Wow. Usually, she manages to fight off the sleeping pills, and that just makes her crankier. I can't believe she slept like that." Marie felt a pang of resentment towards her mother. Did her mother fight off sleep just to mess with Marie and now that there was a nurse, she settled down?

"It happens like that sometimes. Patients

react differently to different people. It's not really a reflection on you, mind, it's just the way it happens. I've read your notes about your days with her, and how you've managed to cope, I'll never know. Especially when she's abusive towards you."

As an employee of the program that paid her to care for her mother 8 hours a day, Marie had to fill out paperwork, make reports and note anything that happened during the hours of her shift. She had to send in copies of it all at the end of the month, but she'd kept the originals at the house. She'd never expected anyone to read them, mainly because nobody ever replied to her about the reports or the notes. Knowing Regina had, embarrassed her a little and she looked way.

"It's not so bad," Marie muttered, too ashamed to look back at the woman.

"It is, but there's nothing you can do about it, and you can't retaliate. It can be hard to deal with, but you seem to cope." Regina's voice was filled with sympathetic understanding. Marie risked a glance up and saw that same sympathy written all over Regina's face.

"It's just how it is," Marie shrugged. She didn't really want to talk about it with anyone, not even Regina.

"Well, if you ever need help, or want to talk, I'm always willing to listen." Regina finished her coffee and stood up. "I need to check on her and do my own report. I'll see you in a bit."

Marie nodded and smiled her gratitude. When she finished her coffee, she went to her room, changed into her normal shorts and t-shirt, and came back out to make breakfast. The air was already hot outside and inside, the temperature started to climb.

She searched around in a drawer until she found a hair clip she kept stashed there and put her hair up. When Regina came back in, bags in hand and ready to go, Marie had a pile of pancakes and bacon ready. "Want some breakfast?"

"Sure, then I really should get home. My husband needs to be up for work in an hour and I have to get my girl off to school."

"Oh, what's your husband do?" It was just small-talk, but it was nice to have someone to talk to in the morning. She could get used to that. The fact that Regina didn't judge her early morning arrival home was nice, too. Marie smiled as she brought maple and blueberry syrup to the table.

"He's a home health nurse too, he just works a different shift, and fewer hours, so one of us can be home with Beth, my daughter." Regina poured the blueberry syrup Marie had made herself over the pan-cakes on her plate and dug in.

"It sounds like a good plan," Marie said, simply to have something to say.

"It works for us. This syrup is beautiful." She took a sip of the orange juice Marie sat in front of her and smiled with pleasure. "So good, all of it."

"Thanks, I made the syrup. The store-bought kind is just too expensive." Marie dug into her own food and the table went quiet.

"Well, thank you for that. I hate to rush, but I really must go now." Regina stood up, gave Marie a wink, and headed for the door. "I hope you have something wonderful planned for tonight. I'll be back around 7:45."

"Oh! For a minute there, I forgot you were coming back! I'll see you then." Marie blinked and stood up with a grateful face. "I can't thank you enough."

"It's my pleasure, Marie. See you tonight."

"Goodbye," Marie called and sat back down. She stared at the now-empty kitchen that would usually make her sad. Today, it didn't.

She might not have had complete sex with Matteo, but it came close. She knew what real pleasure was now, what it felt like to hold a man to your naked skin, and what it was like to sleep beside one. She didn't really care if her mother was a grouch today, she'd had a wonderful night with him. And the promise of an even better night tonight.

She took a deep breath, smiled at the memories they'd made, and then stood up. She was fortified and ready to face her mother now. She walked into the room and saw her mother was still asleep. It seemed all those years of fighting with Marie all night had taken a toll on her. She'd never seen Ruby sleep so peacefully.

Marie decided to leave her to sleep and went to the kitchen to wash up the breakfast dishes. Once she'd finished that, she looked over the calendar and saw she had to pick up some more medicines for her mom today and get the electric bill paid. Back to reality, she thought but smirked her way through it. She didn't care what she had to go through during the day, the nights were all hers now and promised to be worth every moment of grief and the headaches she might get.

15

What she hadn't been prepared for, three mornings ago, was her mother contracting another UTI. She sent Matteo another text to tell him that she wouldn't be able to see him tonight either, even with the nurse there. She couldn't leave her mother when she was that ill.

His text back asked if it was normal for her mother to have so many infections. It wasn't written with anger or suspicion; it was just concern. She wrote back that it could happen, and that she thought her mom would definitely end up in the hospital this time.

"I think it's about time we call for an ambulance and have them take her in for treatment, Marie." Regina came in, her face just as puffy from exhaustion as Marie's was.

"It can take a while for the antibiotics to work with her for some reason, Regina. I'd hate to send her in and then they start working the next day."

"Hmmm." Regina sat down, took the cup of coffee Marie offered her, and sighed. "You should at least get out tonight. I can handle her."

"I just, I don't know. I'm worried she'll try to hit you or something." Marie cringed, ashamed to even have to say that.

"She wouldn't be the first, Marie. She won't be the last." Regina looked at the bruise beneath Marie's eye but didn't ask how she got it. Instead, she smoothed down the bun she'd put her waist-length hair into.

Marie's mind drifted back to earlier

when Ruby had swung her fist at Marie's face just as Marie bent over to change the absorbent pads beneath her mother. The fist had made contact briefly, just enough to bruise Marie's face. Ruby was so out of it with the fever and infection she didn't even know she'd done it.

The fever stayed just high enough to keep Ruby raving, but not high enough to be too dangerous. Marie had to agree with Regina, though, another night of this would be enough. Another one and Marie would call for an ambulance. That's what she told herself anyway.

She knew that the hospital would only prescribe the same antibiotics to Ruby, and they might keep Ruby in to monitor her, but she only had a UTI. The way she acted wasn't an emergency or reason to hospitalize her. It was just... how things were.

Marie had spent the last few nights at home with Regina and Ruby, even though Regina tried to send her out. Marie was terrified that Ruby would go crazy on Regina and hurt her. Marie knew Regina was tough, had experienced a lot over the years, but Marie didn't want Ruby to be yet another patient that had hurt the kind woman. She'd feel so ashamed if that happened.

Marie got another text from Matteo. He hoped Ruby was better soon and asked what he could do to help.

"You've done enough, you sent me Regina, and that's more than I could hope for."

"I hope you get some rest tonight," he sent back. "I miss you, but I know you need to be with your mother."

"Thank you, I'll call you in the morning," she replied.

It was a simple exchange, and neither one mentioned the night they'd shared. Or what they hoped to share in the future. It was all on hold while Marie dealt with the situation. She appreciated that, more than she could tell him.

She went back to the room to find her

mother glaring at Regina slyly. What was she up to?

"Marie, you don't hold a candle to Regina. She doesn't starve me as you do." Ruby watched for Regina's reaction, not Marie's. She was trying to turn Regina against her then. Not a new situation for Marie. She'd often done it in the past if Marie managed to make a friend. Ruby always found a way to run the friend off.

"Mom, you know that's not true."

"Well, what can I say? You're a liar." Ruby threw a rolled-up paper towel at Marie's face, and Marie batted it away.

"You know I'm not, Mom." Marie helped Regina roll Ruby over and replace the absorbent pads beneath the bedridden woman. She pulled Ruby's nightgown down to her hips, replaced her blankets, and gathered up the used pads and paper towels.

It all went into a bag, that went into a trash can with a lid on it. That would all go out in the morning, to the bin outside. A truck came around twice a week, and Marie would take the bin to the road the night before. It was one of the ways Marie worked to keep the house from getting too smelly.

"Do you want your pill now, Ruby?" Regina asked with nothing but kindness, despite the way Ruby treated Marie. Marie had to admire the other woman's calm.

"Yes, I do. Anything that will take my mind off that miserable little sow I gave birth to." Ruby all but spit at Marie as she left the room.

Marie had been embarrassed to let Regina witness how Ruby abused her at first, but now, she didn't even blink.

They'd talked about it over coffee the second morning after Regina started. It had become their routine now, to have a cup of coffee and some breakfast before Regina left. It would be no different tomorrow morning.

Marie poured some coffee into her mug and went into the living room to let Regina deal with Ruby. She only stayed in case Ruby became violent or ranted too much.

From what Regina had observed, it was only Marie that could calm Ruby down when she got too out of touch, but it was also Marie that caused the ranting in the first place. She'd calm down when Marie left the room now, as long as Regina was there. If Marie was on her own, she kept ranting and raving.

She thought about sending Matteo a text, thought about maybe slipping away for a few hours, if her mother actually took the pill. The last few nights, she'd spit the pill out every time they brought it to her. Maybe tonight, she'd take it.

She reached for her coffee and noticed a slight tremor in her hand as she picked it up. She frowned, memories of her mother's hands shaking like that invaded her head and she was overcome with horror. It couldn't be, she finally decided. Parkinson's wasn't generally an inherited disease, especially in women. Then her heart calmed down and she breathed a sigh of relief. That was about her thirteenth cup of coffee for the day. There was little wonder her hands shook!

Regina came in and settled on the other end of the couch. "She's asleep."

"Thank goodness!" Marie breathed a sigh of relief and looked over at Regina. "I can't believe it."

"I think she's as exhausted as you are, dear," Regina reminded her gently that she was able to go home and sleep, Marie was the one that had barely slept in days. "Why don't you go rest? Or go out. You could do with some time away from this place."

"I don't want to leave her," Marie replied, her eyes on the hallway that led to her mother's room. "I wouldn't feel right while she's ill."

Marie hadn't told Regina about Matteo, or what they did, or planned to do, the other woman just knew Marie had a... friend. A good friend that she stayed the night with.

Marie wasn't ready to tell anyone about Matteo, not even Jane. The other woman had come back to work after her own illness earlier that day. She still looked pale and coughed a little, but she was better and back to work.

"Well, at least get some rest while you can. If that coffee in you will let you. Go on, go to bed. I think she's out for the night."

Marie started to protest but knew it was silly to do so. She would fall down and hurt herself if she didn't get some sleep soon. "Alright, you're right. I'll have a shower and then get to sleep."

"Good girl. And I'll make breakfast in the morning. Don't worry about that." Regina shooed Marie on her way, so Marie left with a soft chuckle.

She stood in the shower for a long time, just letting the hot water run over her numb body. She could barely feel anything but aches and pains, but the hot water helped. She cleaned herself before the hot water tank ran out, then got out, just as the spray turned cold.

She picked up her phone, saw that

Matteo had sent a picture, and opened the message up. He was in bed with the top of his silky black pajamas open. Her heart skipped a beat, and then it raced.

She looked up to see the mirror was frosted with steam, so she held the phone out in front of her and snapped her own picture. She had a towel on her head and one around her body, so it wasn't indecent, just... naughty.

She giggled to herself as she left the bathroom and raced for her bedroom. She closed the door quickly and went to her bedroom to send him a text.

"Regina insists I sleep, but I don't want to leave, in case Mom gets worse."

"I understand, and will be busy for the next few moments, so shh!" He'd added a winking emoji and had to smother a laugh.

She wasn't exactly sure what that meant but assumed it had something to do with him taking care of himself, so to speak. "Oh, if you're busy, then you won't want to open this."

She slid the towel around her chest open, just enough to show her cleavage, and snapped a picture. There were still little drops of moisture on her skin, and it looked sexy to her. She quickly sent the picture before she could talk herself out of it, and this time, she got a voice message on her messenger app.

"Mmm," Matteo breathed through a growl. "I can't help myself, Marie. You make me so hard."

She could hear the sound of his hand sliding wetly over something, and knew exactly what he was doing, even if she couldn't see him. But why didn't he just call?

She decided this was a lot more fun, and played the message again. It made her catch her bottom lip between her teeth with excitement and something, down there, went tight deep inside of her.

"Show me," she texted back.

Within seconds a picture appeared, only this one was for her eyes only. She never would have thought seeing a man's erection would turn her on, but now that she saw Matteo's erect cock, well... her mouth started to water.

It glistened in the soft light in the bedroom and was far more colorful than she thought it would be. It was thick and long, at least 9 inches, probably more, and fully erect. She had no idea what it would feel like but knew she'd try to get her hand around it the next time she was with him.

He sent another voice message and she quickly scrambled around for the earbuds that came with the phone. She plugged them in this time, so she could turn it up all the way and hear him properly.

"Marie, I need you so much. You are so fucking hot, baby. I want you here, with me, now. I know you can't be, but fuck." He paused, and she heard that sound again. He was moving that hand of his so fast. "I'm going to take my time with you. I'm going to know every single inch of you before I fuck you, but it might kill me first."

The message ended but another one came right after she'd listened to that one. Her body had already started to respond to his voice. Her nipples were hard little points, her clit throbbed for attention, and deep inside, she ached for him. She didn't know this could happen, but it fascinated her. All he'd done was sent her a voice message, and she was already hungry for him.

"Marie, baby, do you think you could suck my dick? Fuck, I'd love to watch that. Those perfect, sultry lips wrapped around my length." He gave a harsh little sound of pleasure, and she heard the sound of his hand slow down. "I don't want to get off yet, I want to wait for you. To give it to you. But I can't. Fuck, Marie. Fuck!"

A new sound, one that was part defeat, part ultimate gratification, filled her ears and sent a shiver down her body. She knew it was stupid to pant like this, but couldn't help it. She wanted more. She craved him with every fiber of her being. How did she make this stop? Or better? Because it felt so good, she didn't really want it to stop.

A new message came, much longer so it took a moment to load.

"Hi there, baby. Sorry, got carried away. I've waited a long time to do that, and well, I have to say your picture just sent me over the edge. I had to take care of that little problem. But..." he paused here, and she could hear the smirk in his voice, "I suspect it gave you a problem, in return. Give me a call if you want me to help you take care of it."

What did he mean, she wondered? How could he take care of it over the phone? Curious, she dialed his number, with the earbuds in her ears for privacy. He obviously had something he wanted to say to her, and she was more than eager to hear what that was. He didn't answer right away, and the line cut out when he did answer.

Quickly, she hit redial.

16

"Hi, baby," he said when he answered, a growl in his voice that made her shiver all over again. Yeah, she was his, body and soul.

It was a question she'd pondered for a while now. Was she his now? If she was, what was she? That part didn't really matter, but she knew she was his, whether he wanted her or not. He'd woken up this demon in her, now he'd have to take care of it.

"Hi, Matteo," she breathed into the phone, relaxed against her pillows. "How are you going to take care of this, ahem, little problem I have?"

She felt a little silly, talking about sexy stuff like this with him over the phone, but it was fun too.

"Well, you have to be bold, baby. Are your nipples tight?" He asked the question nonchalantly as if the answer didn't matter. But she knew it did.

"Yes," she told him on a gasp. She wasn't ashamed of what they were doing, she just didn't want to be overheard. This was their private business.

"Then pinch them. Pinch them softly." He paused and waited while she did as instructed.

The sensation of her own fingers on her nipples made her gasp. She didn't know it would feel that good to touch her own skin. Her fingers were on the naked flesh of her breasts, tight around the puckered buds on the tips of her breasts. When she groaned he spoke again.

"That sounds so delicious when you

groan like that, Marie. I want you to do something else for me now, alright? I want you to pinch your nipples nice and hard." His voice purred into her head over the line as he guided her. "Imagine it's my fingers, Marie, imagine it's me that's doing that to you."

An image flashed in her head, of her in that virginal white nightgown, with the top down, just enough to bare her breasts to him. A new groan escaped her throat and her fingers gripped even tighter at the tender buds he wanted to touch. Sensations shot around her body and made her head swim, but she didn't want it to end. Not yet.

She stayed like that for at least a minute, maybe longer. He didn't say anything, but she could hear his breath in her ears as she waited for further instructions. She heard a sound from his side of the line like he'd moved around in the bed, and then he spoke.

"Still with me, Marie?" he asked, and she

nodded before she realized he couldn't see that.

"Yes, Matteo." It came out as a whisper; all she could muster at the moment.

"Good. Now I want you to put your phone down and slide your hand down to my pussy."

"My pussy", he'd said. She knew he meant it too. He didn't mean to say hers; he was claiming her most intimate part.

"Find your clit and let me hear your breath as you start to work your fingers over it." His voice was softer, deeper, definitely sensual.

She left the phone just beside her ear and slid her hand into her own wet folds. She gasped when she felt how soaked she really was, how hot her skin was there.

"Mmm, you must be really wet, Marie. Is your finger just sliding around that sweet little clit of yours? Fuck, I want to taste it again so much. I can't forget the taste of you, do you know that? I woke up after you left that morning, and I could still taste your sweet pussy in my mouth, on my hands. Everywhere. I was covered in the taste of you."

Her fingers began to move more quickly, with more pressure, and she found it hard to breathe, but he didn't stop speaking.

"And the way you flooded my mouth when you came, Marie? The sounds you made? Fuck! And that oh so erotic face of yours as you came apart all over me for the very first time? Hang on, I'm hard again already."

She held her breath, listened, as he moved something around, and then the sound of his groan again. She knew what he was doing. What he'd done. He had his cock in his fist again, just from hearing her. From his memory of her.

"That's better, baby. Not as good as having you here, but fuck it, it's all I got."

She didn't know what to say, so she just focused on the sounds that came from his end of the line and worked her hand between her legs. Something was happening there, something she was familiar with now. Something she didn't know she'd needed in her life until he showed it to her.

"You sound so sweet, Marie. I love the way you breathe as your excitement builds." He paused, then groaned a little, which only made her body respond with even more need. She sighed in response to that sound. "Do you remember the feel of my tongue on your skin, Marie?"

A helpless cry tried to break free, but she smothered it. She was supposed to be sleeping, not being naughty with Matteo over the phone.

"I guess you do, baby," his low chuckle told her he was satisfied with his efforts so far.

A need to be his grew within her, nearly strangled her with the fierceness of that desire. She'd never thought she'd be the kind of woman that wanted to belong to a man, but there she was, ready to beg him to make her his in every way possible. He made her feel special, loved, even if he'd never said that word to her. In reality, they barely knew each other. That didn't mean her instincts were wrong, though. He was the one for her, he would make her world complete.

It wasn't the wealth he displayed that drew her, it was the way he looked at her. Like he'd fight against the world just to have her. Something deep inside her responded to that with a need for his protection, for his possession. She knew that she should probably run far, far away from the feelings he evoked, but she couldn't. Instead, she wanted to stoke that need of his, make him take her, make her his.

A new sound shivered out of her, a sound of capitulation, perhaps, and he responded with something deep, guttural, that only made her... *clench.*

"Matteo," she breathed his name, but didn't know if he heard her, she said it so quietly. She wanted him, wanted to go to him, but she needed to stay here, in her bed, working her own clit.

"Come for me, my sweet little darling. Come for me, Marie." His words were a whisper, as light as the sweet stroke of his tongue along her neck. They broke her, though, broke some wall that had built within her a very long time ago, and it all came crashing down around her, as her body exploded.

She said his name, over and over, as the world turned into colored waves of pleasure that left her breathless. She gasped for air in between, tried to tell him to join her, but she couldn't say anything after a while.

Her fingers didn't stop, not even when it became too much, and it started all over again.

"Fuck." She heard him ground out between his teeth. "Fuck. Marie. Baby, I can't stop this. I can't..."

His words broke off as a strangled moan and she knew he was right there with her. He gasped, cried out something that might have been her name, she didn't know, because she was floating all over again, in that peaceful place that he'd given to her. That he'd brought her to.

Moments passed, silent moments of nothing but their breath, the sound of her own heartbeat as her heart slammed in her chest. It felt like it wanted to pound right out of her body, but it soon calmed, until all she heard was his breath.

"Matteo?" she prompted, even though she wanted to remain in her bliss.

"I'm okay, Marie. Sleep baby. You deserve it. I'll stay on the line, just in case you wake up and want me."

She couldn't help the smile on her face or the way she curled up in her small twin bed, content for now. She left the earbuds in her ears and fell into her dreams, his breath there to remind her that she was safe. For now.

MARIE WOKE up the next morning, rested and ready for the day. Her earbuds had come out of her ears, and her phone was almost dead, so she went to the kitchen to connect it to the charger. She found Regina there, with gravy and biscuits ready and on the table.

"Good morning! I was about to wake you." Regina was her normal chipper self, and Marie couldn't help but respond to that.

"I must have smelled this." She looked up from her seat at the table and smiled. "You didn't have to do all of this. You've had a rough night, I'm sure."

"Actually, I think your Mom is coming around. She went to sleep around two a.m. and has been snoozing away ever since."

"I can't believe it." Marie was surprised but pleased. Maybe that was good news, then? "Has her fever broken?"

"It was down when I checked it at midnight. Let's hope she's out of the woods."

"I hope so. It's been rough." Marie broke up her biscuits, put a fried egg on top, then smothered it all in gravy. Not the usual way to eat the dish, but that's how she liked it.

She added a piece of sausage to her plate and dug in. Regina would have to get home soon and Marie didn't want to keep her. Her excursions the night before must have drained her energy, because she ended up eating an extra biscuit with a piece of sausage stuffed into it as Regina left.

"See you tonight." Regina waved and left through the backdoor.

Marie went to her mother's room, checked on her, and saw that she was still asleep. Ruby's skin felt cool to the touch, for the first time in days, and she didn't whimper in her sleep, as she'd done the few moments she'd actually slept. Marie knew Ruby was on the road to recovery now, and the relief she felt almost dropped her to the floor.

Hopefully, the ranting and raving would be over now.

Marie went to the bathroom had a quick shower and dressed in her usual attire. A clean pair of shorts, a bright green t-shirt, and her hair down to dry. She checked on her mother one more time, then went to the kitchen to clean it up. She put the radio on and hummed along to it as she washed the dishes up.

Her phone chirped, and she quickly dried her hands to see what it said. Only one person knew her phone number, so she didn't doubt who it was from.

"How's your mother?" the text asked.

"She's asleep, her fever's gone, and she's peaceful," Marie added a smiling emoji and sent the text. She leaned back against the counter as she waited for his reply.

"Meet you at the café?" Matteo sent.

"I'll be there." She gave a laugh of happiness and sent the text.

Her mother spent the morning and early afternoon asleep. She hated to think it, but Marie was relieved. Her mother had been a holy terror to everyone throughout this latest illness, and they all needed a break from her. Marie was supposed to get a break now, Matteo had generously seen to that, but she was too devoted to leave Regina alone with Ruby. Marie wasn't quite sure if that devotion was to Regina or her mother.

Since she'd met Matteo, she'd spent a lot of time thinking about the last few years of her life. About her entire life, really. It had not been easy, some would say it was even Hell, but it was all she'd known. She'd put up with a lot, fought back when she could, and had learned to pick her battles. If nothing else, her mother taught her to know which battles were worth fighting for.

By the time Jane arrived, Marie was ready to head out the door. She greeted the other woman, asked about her health, and then quietly slipped out of the door. There were no medicines to pick up today, she didn't need any shopping, and all she wanted was to see Matteo. She drove to the café with the radio off, it jangled her nerves too much, so she turned it off to have some peace.

Over the last few days, her mother had spent her days screaming about demons, and how Marie was the daughter of Satan and not really Ruby's child. She'd ignored most of it when she was alone with Ruby, but if Jane or Regina was present, her mother's raving caused her shame. What must these nice ladies think of her, if her own mother talked about her like that?

It was hard. Ruby made it harder, but she'd got through it. Matteo's memory, his phone calls, and texts had helped her immensely, and she planned to tell him that when she saw him. She pulled into the parking lot, got out, and looked around.

He hadn't arrived yet, so she ordered her usual coffee and beignets, and found a table towards the back of the sitting area. She'd finished her snack when he pulled into the parking lot, the engine of his classic car a vibrating roar that made her grin. She wanted to take a ride in it, sometime. She'd have to remember to ask him.

He got out of the car, a cocky smile on that face of his as he loped towards her. His stride ate up the distance and instead of sitting down with her, he pulled her up out of her seat and towards the side of the building, where trees would block anyone from spotting them.

He pushed his glasses up, and the hunger in his eyes set her on fire. Before she could say a word, his lips were fused to hers, and his hands were on her ass. The press of his fingers there tilted her hips towards him, and she felt him, hard and ready for her. He broke away, and she felt the heat of his skin as his lips slid to her left ear.

"I'd fuck you right here, against this wall, but you deserve better than that, Marie. But, you need to know, I want you more than I've ever wanted any other woman on this planet." He pressed his erection into her and all she could do was whimper as she looked up into eyes that burned for only her.

"I might be able to come to your house tonight," she said after a moment, even though her lips felt oddly numb and her brain could barely churn out a coherent thought. He was too close, too aroused, and it made her brain scatter. All she knew was she wanted whatever he wanted, and she'd let him have her against this wall if that's what he wanted.

"Fuck, I hope you do, Marie. I need you so much." His fingers tensed on her ass again, and she moaned into his mouth. He inhaled the sound as if it was the most wonderful nectar he'd ever tasted. "I can't take too much more of this."

"I...," she started to speak but he pulled away, his self-assured grin back in place. She wanted to trace the outline of his lips with her fingers but held herself still. This was a man on the edge, and she didn't want to push him, not here, anyway. "Want some coffee?"

"No, but I'll take some." His laugh soothed the frantic beat of her heart, and the way he clasped her hand in his as he took her back to her seat made her feel warm. It was a nice kind of warm, the kind that came from somewhere inside and might be called happiness.

They had 30 minutes. It was enough for now. At least he hadn't mentioned the bruise on her face. For a little while, she even forgot about it being there.

17

"I can deal with her, Marie. This is my job, remember? I'm trained to handle cases like this. Now, it's been at least a week since you've had a good night's sleep with that *friend* of yours, I suggest you go see, ahem, *them.*" Regina glared at Marie across the kitchen table and sealed her lips together.

Marie knew that meant she wasn't going to say another word, and she'd just have to do as Regina said. The woman was stubborn, that's for sure, Marie thought as she stood up from the table, her face doubtful.

"Fine. She's nicer to you anyway." Marie

turned to leave but then turned back. "If you need me…"

"I have your number. Now, go, get out of here." Regina waved her hands around until Marie moved towards the door.

Marie got in the car and drove down the road. When she was halfway into town, she pulled into a gas station that also served food and sent Matteo a text. The afternoon had been hell and she kind of dreaded seeing him.

She glanced up in the rearview mirror, and with the help of the overhead lights of the gas station looked at her face. A bruise, and a cut. She hadn't been able to get the nail scissors off the table fast enough. She'd cut her mother's nails while she was asleep, but Ruby woke up before Marie could put them away. She'd immediately complained that she was wet, and Marie had instantly got up to change the pads and clean her mother up.

"Where have you been, Marie? I can smell a man on you. What have you been up to, you, you little slut?" Ruby's angry voice and her words stopped Marie cold. Ruby had obviously forgotten the night Marie told her a man was interested in her. Marie had been happy that her mother forgot, but somehow, she sensed Matteo on her now. How?

Marie went back to rolling her mother around and decided to lie. "There's no man, Momma. It's just the cologne from the pharmacy. Netty was spraying it around again."

"Bullshit. That's expensive cologne I smell on you. And something else. Sweat? What have you been doing? Tell me, dammit!" Ruby pushed herself up, her eyes full of righteous anger, and Marie pulled back. She wasn't fast enough, and she felt the sharp slice of the nails scissors before she even saw her mother's hand move. "That's what sluts get!"

Instead of running off screaming like she wanted to, Marie controlled herself. She'd learned the technique a long time ago.

Stay calm, don't overreact, don't be defensive, just deflect until you can get the weapon and get out of the way.

"Momma, there's no man, now calm down." Marie stood tall over her mother, reached for the scissors with one hand, and held her mother down gently with the other. The sick woman was so weak, it didn't take much.

Marie could feel the drip of blood as it ran down her face, but she didn't even swipe at it. She continued her task, ignored the enraged shrieks of her mother, and then cleared away the garbage and the washtub. She cleaned the tub out, put it up, washed her hands, and then took a moment to look at herself in the bathroom mirror.

It wasn't much, a scratch more than anything, but it would probably leave a small scar for a while. She cleaned it off, swiped some antibiotic ointment on it, then went to check on Ruby. She'd calmed down, but she glared at Marie with pure hatred.

"You're going to end up just like me. I

knew you were rotten. I should have aborted you before I even told your father about you." There was nothing but venom on Ruby's twisted, wrinkled face. A face that was ruined by self-loathing and decades of self-abuse. Marie sighed and turned away.

The insult didn't sting anymore, not like it used to anyway. Marie looked away from the rear-view mirror and waited for Matteo to text back. He'd wanted to take her out to eat, but she couldn't, not with a bruise under her eye and a cut under the other. People would think he did it.

"Sure, we can stay at the house, if you want. Swim, watch movies, whatever you want to do." His text came back quick enough, and she took a deep breath with relief. She hadn't told him how the rest of the day had gone yet.

She'd told him about her mother's illness, and how it made her delusional, but she hadn't quite told him the full extent of it. He'd seen the bruise today, but he hadn't questioned her. His jaw had tightened when he got a good look at it, but he didn't ask her how it happened. He was bound to ask now.

She didn't like to admit to anyone that her mother was abusive, much less violent. There was no way to hide this, though. She could tell him it was accidental, that her mother had a nightmare that she was a monster or something and struck out at her. But she didn't want to lie to Matteo, not even to protect her mother. Not even to spare herself the shame of it all.

Because the truth was, Marie had walked around with black eyes long before her mother's illness had developed. Ruby had physically abused Marie since she could remember. It was an everyday thing for her. Usually, the bruises were hidden, but sometimes, Ruby would mess up if she was drunk, or high, and Marie would have yet another black eye.

Normally, she kept the thought at bay, the thoughts about what she'd endured, but it was getting harder to stay with her mother. Marie knew she was ill, Marie knew she needed her daughter's help, but this was getting out of control. And what would Matteo think?

Fuck, this was starting to get too difficult, she thought as she turned down the road that took her to his house. She dreaded seeing his face, the anger that would likely make his jaw go tight again, as his eyes narrowed. But maybe he wouldn't notice. Maybe he'd think she'd fallen or something.

That's what she'd told the teachers at school. And the social workers. And the police. She'd told them all different stories over the years. A rock had spun up and hit her in the face when she mowed the grass. She'd fallen and hit her face on the edge of the steps to the backdoor. She'd tripped and hit the edge of the footboard of her bed. She'd, she'd, she'd. She'd always taken the blame, even though it was Ruby's fault.

Maybe it was time to stop that and tell someone the truth?

With a resigned frown, Marie turned her car off and headed up the steps to Matteo's house. It was time to face him and get it over with. That was something else her mother taught her: face your problems, deal with them, then prepare for the next set of problems, because more was always on the way. Not the happiest outlook on life, but it had kept her prepared, anyway.

Matteo answered the door, a smile in place, and his eyes glittered in the dark. He took in the cut under her eye, the bruise under the other, and instead of questioning her, or being angry, or anything that might make the tears in her eyes spill from her lids, he took her in his arms and held her gently. He inhaled her scent, just like she inhaled his, and the tears fell, even though she tried to stop them. He let her cry, he didn't scream at her about what the neighbors might think or try to drag her into the house, he just let her cry on him for a long few minutes.

"You're tired baby, and obviously upset. Do you want to sit down? I can have someone bring you a drink or something to eat if you want?" He hadn't pulled away or tried to push her down to the step, he'd just talked softly, soothingly, as his hands ran up and down her back to comfort her.

She pulled away, embarrassed at what she'd just done. "Wow, I'm so sorry about that. I don't know what came over me."

"You're doing a very hard job, Marie, you're going to have moments like this. It's bound to happen. I'm just glad I can be here for you." He pulled back a little, dried the tears in her eyes, and handed her a hand-kerchief out of his pocket. What man carried those now, she thought stupidly as she dried her nose on the clean cloth.

"I'm really sorry about that, Matteo. I just lost it, I guess. I'm so sorry." She turned around, to stare out at the luxury of his spacious front yard. She didn't really see it, she was just trying to get ahold of herself.

He pulled her back to face him and looked at her with uncertainty. Then, he seemed to make his mind up. "Come into the house, let's watch a movie, and you can have whatever you want. You don't have to talk if you don't want to, or we can spend the entire night talking, whatever you want, Marie."

"A movie sounds good." She followed him into the house and tried to hide the sounds of her sniffles. She swiped at her nose again and wondered if he'd want the handkerchief back once she washed it?

And just like that, she was alright. He didn't make a big deal out of it, even though she could see he wanted to, he just did what he had to do to give her the space she needed. She adored him for that far more than she would have if he'd gone off angry and made some kind of demands about her mother. There was nothing that could be done anyway.

They found a movie to watch and sprawled out on the couch together. Only a few hours before they'd been desperate to get each other naked, but that had all changed when she walked up to the house. She needed comfort, a friend more than a lover, and Matteo offered her that. That was worth more than anything to Marie at that moment.

She leaned into his chest, comfortable and content. She'd never actually had this kind of human contact before Matteo came along. Her mother had barely held her as a baby, and when she grew into a toddler, refused to pick her up at all. Her first memories were of her mother slapping her. She'd fallen, scraped her knee, and wanted comfort. She'd soon learned not to do that again.

To lie next to him like this, again, was more than a treat, it was… heaven. His arm was around her, and she held his other hand with hers, over his chest. His arm was probably numb by now, but he didn't seem to mind. He just held her and let her rest there with him.

When the movie finished, he asked what she wanted to do next. She thought about it, and then asked him something that made him grin.

"Do you have any floats for that pool of yours?" She sat up and looked down at him. He was in a relaxed mood, with a pair of dark blue pajama bottoms and a t-shirt on. To her, it was one of the sexiest outfits he could wear.

"I do, actually. Want to swim?" He sat up too, turned the TV off, and stood up. "I can get a bottle of wine and put on some music."

"Actually, do you have any beer? I've never had it. I'd like to see what all the fuss is about."

"I do indeed," he said with an amused chuckle.

"And a radio? There's this channel I like. I thought it might be nice to float in the pool, spend some time staring up at the stars, and just listen to some music."

"As long as the mosquitoes don't carry you away. Or the frogs. I don't know how people can stand that."

"Ah, you're a city boy. I forgot for a minute." She knew he came from somewhere up in New York City, but she wasn't sure where exactly. "I guess you're used to traffic noise and bars, but not frogs."

"Nope. Never heard the things until I came down here." They walked into the kitchen where he grabbed a 6-pack of something that looked expensive, a small radio, and headed out towards the pool. She followed along, trying to decide whether it was a good idea to swim naked or not.

Could she take her clothes off in front of him? She wasn't sure she was brave enough, but she was about to find out. He handed her the battery-operated radio and she tuned it to the right station. Cajun music filled the air as he went into the little cabin to get her a float.

She put the radio down and decided that maybe if she hurried up and got in the water, she could do it. She stripped down quickly and all but ran into the water. She ran so fast, she was over her head before she knew it, and came up for air to find him standing at the side of the pool, in a pair of shorts, with a very amused tilt to his eyebrow.

"Hot, were you?" he asked, and his voice dripped with the same amusement that showed in that raven eyebrow of his.

"Just a little," she said with her head up, proud and unapologetic. "I might have been a little too eager, but here we are. Two grown people, swimming in the dark."

"Well, you're the only one swimming. And if I had to guess, I'd say you're swimming naked."

"I might be." She didn't let her head drop at all, determined to play this amusing little game. She tried not to grin and almost failed, but she looked away from him and saved herself. "Is that a problem?"

"Not at all, Miss Hebert. Suit yourself, I say." He came down into the water, two floats in his arms, and slid one out to where she was. "If you want to climb up on that, you're more than welcome to."

"I think I might." His eyes dared her to, and she wasn't about to back down now. She'd got this far, she might as well play along. She went to the shallow end, while he floated out to the deep end. The only light came from below, and there wasn't anyone else around to see her.

She told herself that they both knew he'd see her completely naked eventually, so she might as well get on that float and ride it like she was the Queen of Sheba herself. Besides, the man had slid his tongue all over her intimate parts. If he'd been disgusted by her body, he'd have said something by now.

She cast a glance in his direction, only to find he wasn't facing her at all. He knew she was being brave and had decided to make it easier for her then. That or he was totally oblivious. She knew at least one thing about

Matteo, oblivious he was not. He was being respectful. Again.

It nearly made her tear up, but she pushed that down. With a nervous giggle, she managed to get on the float and settle against the backrest without rolling it over. A splash caught her attention and she saw Matteo had made his way to the edge of the pool where he'd left the beer. He pulled two out and faced her.

For a moment, he looked her over, and she saw the way his eyes narrowed, the way his lips parted, and his eyebrows went up. Only this time, it was with appreciation, not amusement. His float drifted by hers, and he handed her a bottle of cold beer.

"For you, my dear," he offered.

"Thank you, kindly," she responded, and let out a calm sigh. "Okay, this is good. This is really good."

"I'm glad you approve. Now, float along, drink your beer, and relax, Marie. That's all you have to do."

So that's what she did.

18

"It's time to wake up, Marie." Matteo's voice, an echo somewhere in the darkness, pulled her from the warm place she was cocooned in. She wanted to push his voice away, to stay in this peaceful place for a little while longer. Besides, he was there with her, wasn't he?

Marie blinked, uncertain about what was happening. Then she remembered. She was in Matteo's bed. They'd spent the evening in the pool, drinking, listening to music, and staring up at the stars from their floats. She's relaxed in the magical atmosphere and held his hand as they floated together, their eyes on the stars.

When the third bottle of beer made her tipsy, he'd tugged her out of the pool, dried her off, then sent her into the bathroom to shower off. When she'd come out, he'd guided her to the bed, and they'd talked. Only talked. Well, she talked, and he listened.

She'd told him about how she'd wanted to go back to school to become a doctor, how she'd had it all planned out. She was going to escape this place, and never come back. That was before she knew her mother was ill. She didn't go into detail about the abuse she'd taken as a child, or what went on now, she didn't want to change the mood, or make him think she wanted him to feel sorry for her. She didn't want that at all, so she kept that part to herself.

She'd gone quiet then and must have fallen asleep. His warm body was pressed into hers, and she turned into his arms.

"I don't want to get up." She sighed

against his neck, determined to stay hidden there, under his head, for the rest of the day. Her mother would have to find someone else to abuse today, she'd had about enough of it. And the problem was only growing worse. She didn't want to be hit anymore or screamed at, or demeaned by the one person in this world that was supposed to love her unconditionally. She wanted to stay right here, where she was safe and perhaps even loved.

"I know you don't want to go home, and I really don't want you to get up, but you have to. You have to let Regina go home."

"I don't want to!" She murmured it louder and clasped her arm around his waist and threw a leg over his hip for good measure.

"I know, Marie, and I don't blame you. But you have to go. You'll hate yourself if something happens to her and you aren't there." There was a weight to his words that made her look up at him sharply.

"What happened?" It was instinct alone that made her ask that question.

"I went to Italy to study for a couple of years, right after I turned 18. I thought I had time, you know? I didn't go home once in all that time, because I was enjoying myself too much. Mom was only 38, she'd had a cough for a very long time, but she said it was only allergies. We didn't worry about it. Mom just... coughed a lot." His voice trailed off on a note of strangled pain. He took a deep breath, tightened his arms around her, and continued. "She found out she had cancer a month before she died. She'd started chemo, all the things she was supposed to do, and she told me to stay in Italy. I had two more months before I was supposed to come back home, so she told me to stay, that she'd be fine."

"But she wasn't?" Marie prodded when he went silent again. She didn't want to cause him more pain, but she wanted him to continue. He so rarely talked about himself, about his personal life, that she didn't want him to stop.

"The cancer had spread over the years, all around her lungs, down into her abdomen. It spread into her lower aorta and caused massive internal bleeding. She bled out before the doctors at the hospital could stop it. I never got to see her again." His voice was thick by that time, full of raw pain that he held at bay.

Marie's fingers tightened on him, an involuntary movement to bring him closer, to ease his pain. She turned her face, kissed his jaw, and held him as the quiet moment went on. "I'm so sorry you never got to see her again."

"I am too, which is why I'm pushing you out of this bed and on your way home." He got out of the bed suddenly and clapped his hands. "Out you go, Marie. Let's get the day started."

His smile was a little wobbly, but his eyes were clear, and his body relaxed. He'd brushed off his own pain and focused on her. It made Marie wonder if she'd ever stop melting over him. She put on a brave smile and slid out of the bed.

"Fine," she said as she pulled her hair into a bun and secured it with the hair tie she'd left on the bedside table. "I guess I should get home."

"Yep. I'll see you later this evening, and you can tell me how your day was. I'll text you later." He kissed her and disappeared down the hall.

She found the other bathroom he'd shown her and cleaned up a little. She had her own toothpaste and toothbrush in here; her own shower products, and towels. It was kind of nice to know she had her own things at his house.

He'd left by the time she walked out the door and got in her car. Light slanted along the top of the trees and straight at her face as she got behind the wheel. She flicked down the sun visor, but it didn't really help. This was the only thing she hated about mornings, driving in that bright sunlight that blinded her, yet left other places so very dark.

She made it home in time to let Regina give her the rundown of the previous night and say goodbye. Her mother had slept, again, thankfully. She was still asleep, so Marie went into her bedroom, changed clothes, and put a load of dirty clothes in the washer. She spent the morning in the laundry room and folded loads as they came out of the dryer. By the time Jane showed up, the table was full of clothes, bed linens, and towels.

"You've had a busy morning." The cheerful face of the nurse came into view around the edge of the doorframe and Marie smiled in greeting.

"I have, but it's all clean now, I think." It was a task she didn't mind doing; it helped her to relax, even though the folding was physical work.

"Good, where are you off to today?"

"I have to go to the library, the grocery

store, and stop by the pharmacy. No coffee and beignets today, I'm afraid."

"Well, don't rush too much. I'll be here, so she's in good hands."

Marie nodded her thanks and left the laundry room. She went by the library first, found a new stack of books, and then went to the pharmacy. The insurance company had given the pharmacist a fit over one of her mother's medicines, so Marie used her new phone to call them. She'd sometimes have to use the one at the pharmacy to make these calls, but she had her own now and got the matter sorted quickly.

She then made her way to the store. She noticed a few open stares from staff members, and a few other customers, but ignored them. She was used to being blanked and knew there must be rumors going around about her relationship with Matteo. She could almost imagine them all tittering to each other about it.

"What does he see in her?" one would say, without knowing Marie at all. They only

knew the rumors. Some might remember her from school, but even back then, nobody had spoken to her.

"She's a slut, just like her mother was," another might say, probably the slighted wife of one of Ruby's former conquests.

"She's only after his money. Her mother was money-hungry too until karma bit her in the ass and made her sick," another bitter rival might say.

They were all things she'd heard, in one fashion or another, before. People were mean, snide, and downright snotty. Marie had stopped wondering why a long time ago. They didn't know her, and never would because her mother made sure they were both outcasts. Marie didn't care, she decided as she slung a box of cereal into the cart and went down to the dairy section. The people that stared, and their opinions, really didn't matter to her at all.

The only person that really mattered was Matteo, and she was sure he'd been warned about her by someone already.

Some busybody would have warned him, with a knowing stare, to stay away from Marie Hebert. They might have even added in that she was no good.

He didn't seem to care, though, so she didn't either. Fuck them and their opinions.

She went home, spent a few minutes with Jane, and then went into her mother's bedroom. Her mother's eyes narrowed when she saw the marks on Marie's face, and a look of guilt swept over her features. It wasn't there for long, but Marie saw it.

That look confused her. Her mother never said she was sorry, never apologized for anything. She didn't promise to never hit or scream at Marie again. She just did as she pleased, with no regrets. But Marie could have sworn she saw it there on her mother's face, even if it hadn't lasted very long.

"Out slutting around again were you?"

"Oh, yes, Momma. I slutted it up with the pharmacist, with the butcher at the grocery store, and then, for good measure, I did more slutting over at the library with the pretty new librarian." Marie wasn't sure what exactly had come over her, but she didn't question it too much. Matteo had given her strength, shown her she had worth, and now, she would use that strength to help her get through this time with her mother.

"That's not funny, Marie. It's not funny at all. Where's my lunch?" Ruby glared at her daughter. Her brows knit together when Marie didn't flinch or hang her head.

Marie saw the confusion and smiled even more. "I thought it was funny, Momma. Your lunch will be ready in five minutes. I'll see if I can find someone else to slut with while I prepare it."

"That's about enough of your smart mouth, Marie," Ruby shouted as Marie laughed and walked away.

"I'm sure it is, Momma," Marie shouted back. She would probably regret being smart with her mother. Her mother would find a way to make her pay, but she didn't care. It was worth it to see her mother so uncertain and maybe even a little worried that she'd lost the upper hand.

Ruby had always been a calculating woman, and she'd used every weapon in her arsenal on Marie, and everyone else she came into contact with over the years. Now, Marie was turning the tables. Ruby would just have to get used to this new, confident daughter, whether she liked it or not.

Marie fed Ruby, gave her a bed bath, and then put the television on for her. The day was a little cooler, so she turned the AC down and made sure her mother had enough blankets on the bed. "I'm going to wash up the dishes, Mom. Call me if you need me."

Ruby muttered something that Marie couldn't hear, but Marie didn't rise to the bait. She just left the room and went into the kitchen. She checked her phone and saw that Matteo had sent her a link to a high-end, very expensive looking, clothing shop.

"I'm in New Orleans and saw this dress in a shop window. What size and color do you want?" the next text said.

Marie blinked at the phone. There wasn't even a price on the thing, just the possible sizes and colors.

"I would need a medium, I guess," she wrote to him. "Red?"

"Red would be perfect. I'll see you tonight. I'm taking you out. The dress will be delivered to your house."

Marie touched her face, felt the cut on one side and the bruise on the other. She couldn't go out in public with her face like this. Surely, he knew that?

19

The dress came in a delivery van marked with the store's insignia. A large white box tied with a sapphire blue silk bow. Marie tugged at the bow and examined the material. It really was silk.

Alone in her bedroom, she gaped at the box, at the bow, and wondered how much Matteo had spent on the dress. Luxury oozed from every part of the gift box. Even the box itself was some thick cardboard that made her think of the word "cardstock". She wasn't quite sure what it meant but she must have read it somewhere, she decided.

After a few more breaths, she pulled the lid off the box and pushed blue tissue paper aside. It was a red silk dress, a wrap-around dress with a v-neck and silky, shiny satin around the edges. She pulled it from the box and found it had flirty cap sleeves and the hem came down to around mid-calf. Flirty, sexy, but still slightly demure. Like her, she thought as she held it up to her body and looked at herself in the mirror on the back of her bedroom door.

There was another box too, one that held a pair of black heels and lingerie far more beautiful than anything she owned. There was even a slip inside the box, pale pink and delicate. Everything she'd need for a night out.

She put the dress down, picked up her phone, and wrote a message.

"You can't take me anywhere looking like I do right now."

She deleted it and wrote another.

"You don't want to take me out in public, I don't know to put makeup on."

That one didn't sound right to her either, so she pressed the back button until it was gone.

"Are you sure you want to be seen in public with me?"

She didn't feel too good about that one either, but it was the truth of the matter. She wasn't sure Matteo would like the whispers or the looks that would follow if he took her out in this town. She hit send.

"A woman is coming at 7 to do your hair and makeup. If you don't want the makeup that's fine but let her do your hair at least. You'll enjoy the experience, I promise."

His text made her laugh, but it was an awkward laugh. Of course, he'd thought of everything. He always would, though, he was just that kind of man.

She took a shower, dried her hair, and by 7, she was at the kitchen table waiting for this mystery woman to show up. A knock at the door signaled that she was there, and Marie went to the door to let her in.

"Hi, I'm Amy. I'm here to get you ready for your date."

"Marie! Marie, who's here?" The question was more of a demand from her mother than an inquiry.

"It's for me, Mom. Don't worry." Marie waited a moment, listened, but didn't hear anything else.

"Come in, Amy. I'm Marie, obviously." Marie led the black-haired woman with sharp blue eyes into the living room. "Where do you want to do this?"

Amy shut the door and looked around. "Is there more light in the kitchen?"

"There is." Marie nodded, not sure what else she should say.

"Let's go in there."

Marie took Amy into the kitchen and sat down at the table. She saw the woman had several bags and boxes with straps on her shoulder. Amy placed those on the table, and Marie noticed that the woman was tall, slim, and dressed all in black. It looked good on her, but Marie wasn't sure she could pull it off.

"Alright, let me know what you like? Up, down, curly, straight?" Amy stood behind Marie and pulled at her hair. The locks were shiny, healthy, and long, but straight as a board.

"I've never had my hair done, I don't know."

"What's the dress look like?" Amy asked and Marie picked up her phone to show her the picture Matteo sent.

"Hm. Up, I think. You don't want to hide the dress with all this gorgeous hair," Amy said and then got to work. She plugged in curlers, straighteners, and pulled out several bottles of stuff Marie didn't recognize. Then she took out pins and a few other fasteners before she opened the boxes.

"Now, I think, as you're such a lovely lady, all we really need to do is camouflage that bruise and the cut and highlight those amazing eyes of yours." Amy turned Marie to look at her face more closely. "God, you've got gorgeous skin."

"Thanks." Marie felt her cheeks go red and looked down. "I don't know anything about hair or makeup, so I'm at your mercy really."

"Don't worry, you're in good hands. I won't overdo it, you don't need much, really."

"Thank you," Marie whispered it this time and wondered how long it would all take.

Amy started to explain everything she did, as she did it, and all Marie could do was agree. "These are all samples," she added as she went along, "so you can keep what's left."

"Oh, okay. Thanks," Marie said as Amy sponged something over the bruise below her eye.

Something else went on the cut, and then Amy sponged something different from that across Marie's skin. Marie started to wonder if her skin would be visible at all when this was all done. There seemed to be a lot of blending, sponging, and more blending going on than she'd like, but she did have two places to hide.

The makeup around her eyes might have been the most difficult part. She had to sit with her eyes closed as Amy daubed, lined, and then daubed some more. Mascara went on, and Amy finally stepped back. It had only taken ten minutes but felt like an hour to Marie. Amy nodded and then held up a mirror.

Marie's eyes went wide as she looked at herself. She was... pretty! "Wow!"

"Thanks, stunned was the reaction I was hoping for." Amy smiled and nodded her head happily. "Let's do your hair."

Amy sprayed, curled, pinned, and then curled some more. Marie winced a few times as the curler pulled at her hair, but it was mostly just a matter of waiting. Amy looked one last time, moved a curl, and sprayed. "That's it, I think."

She held up a mirror and Marie gasped all over again. "That's all my hair?"

"It's all yours." Amy had pinned Marie's hair up into a loose chignon, curled the ends into a swirly cascade, and left a few romantic tendrils to rest against her cheeks.

The look wasn't overdone at all. It was romantic, sensual, and Marie couldn't believe it was her! "Thank you so much. I definitely couldn't have done this."

Marie couldn't stop looking in the mirror, but a knock at the door said it was time for Marie to dress and go. Regina walked in but stopped as soon as she saw Marie.

"Wow!" She drew the word out on a long syllable. "You are gorgeous!"

"Oh hush." Marie ducked her head down, but was pleased with Regina's reaction.

"No, really. You're beautiful anyway but like that? You're just, wow. I feel like a proud mom on her daughter's wedding day."

Regina choked up a little and her eyes glistened.

"Aw, Regina, thank you!" Marie took her hand, and Amy started to pack up.

"My job here is done. I hope you have a lovely evening, Marie, and take care. I've left my card if you need anything or would like to have me work on you again."

"I just might," Marie said with a smile and thanked the woman one last time.

"Well, then, my gorgeous little friend, get dressed and get out of here. I'll take over from here."

"Alright. I have no idea what we're doing, but it's obviously something special. I'll go get my dress on."

Marie hurried into her bedroom, put on her new panties, pink to match the slip, slid the dress over the new slip, and pushed her feet into the heels. She turned to look at herself in the mirror and forgot how to breathe.

That couldn't be her. That woman was grown, she was beautiful. It wasn't her at all, was it? Marie stepped closer, looked at her face and body in the dress, but couldn't believe it was really her. She was really... pretty.

She'd never been conceited and didn't want to think the word gorgeous, but when she looked at her reflection in the mirror, she saw a woman that could be in magazines. How had that happened?

"It was all Amy's work," she said to herself and stepped back. "I don't really look like that."

But she did, and she couldn't help the smile that spread over her face. She dabbed the small sample of lipstick over her lips and went out to greet Regina. "I'm off now."

"Baby girl, whoa..." Regina was speechless after that.

"It's good?"

"It's more than good, Marie. It's exactly what you deserve, honey. I'm just..." She stopped, her eyes full of happy tears again.

"I'm so pleased for you. This is what you deserve. A man that does this for you."

"He's done well," Marie had to agree and picked up her bag. "I'll see you in the morning, I guess. Have the coffee on, and I'll tell you how the night goes."

"I'll be waiting patiently. I hope it's as lovely as you are, Marie, your night that is. Have fun, sweety." Regina stepped up to Marie, kissed her cheek softly, and pulled away. "Have *fun*!"

"I will. Thank you." Marie clasped Regina's hand and then left the house.

She drove over to Matteo's and met him at the door.

"You ready to go?" he asked and then stepped out to get a better look at her.

His jaw dropped open and he stared at her.

"Is it too much?" She'd been terrified on the way over, worried if he'd hate it, or love this new look of hers. It wasn't like it would happen often, but she wanted him to like it anyway. He'd paid to have it all done, after all.

"It's, fucking hell, Marie. She's done magic. Don't get me wrong, honey, you're always gorgeous, with or without makeup and the hair, but you are stunning."

Marie could feel the way her face glowed with pride and could but feel a light of happiness beaming out of her head. Matteo approved and that was what mattered the most.

Matteo continued to stare at her and she laughed.

"Well, are we just staying out here in the dark all night?"

"What?" he asked and blinked. "Oh, no, let's get in the car. I'm taking you to New Orleans."

"Alright." She was happy to hear they wouldn't be going somewhere in town; she was a little overdressed. She noticed, at last, that he had on a tailored black suit, made of a fine, lightweight material. Moonlight glinted off the silky darkness of his hair as he sat forward and started the car.

The engine roared to life and Marie's eyes opened a little more. She could feel the engine through her seat and the vibration made her giggle.

"Like it?" he asked, a grin on his face.

"I do." She nodded and looked at the car. The sound system had been updated, and he'd had a navigation system installed, but everything else was original to the car and full of the promise of luxury. She'd never been in a car so sexy before, and when he put the gear shift in first gear and pulled out, her heart raced with excitement.

It was a sports car and every inch of it was made for speed. They raced down the road, on their way to the glittering lights of New Orleans that beckoned in the distance.

She was quiet as they drove, happy to enjoy the ride, and looked out as they crossed over the Bonnet Carre Spillway. It was always romantic in the dark, and she couldn't help the smile that spread over her face.

Everything about Matteo made her smile. Just being with him made her smile; the things he did, the way he adored her, everything made her smile. He hadn't done any of this to impress her, she knew that without him saying a word. He'd done this because he wanted to make her happy, and he'd succeeded so far.

It hadn't occurred to her to refuse his gifts, she hadn't even protested, she thought as they left the spillway behind and drove on. He wanted to give her the things she didn't have, to give her the things he thought she deserved. Not to show off, or impress on her that he was rich, but because he thought she should have whatever she needed or wanted.

How had she gotten so lucky, after a lifetime of misery?

"Thank you, Matteo," she said softly, but loud enough that he could hear her.

"It was my pleasure, Marie." He took her

hand, kissed the back of it, and then frowned. "You don't have any jewelry?"

"No. Costs too much, even for the cheap stuff." She looked down at her hand. "Besides, your hand on mine is decoration enough."

"Maybe so," he said and kissed her hand again. He let go to change gears and then pulled off an exit.

He drove easily through the streets, as if he'd grown up in the area, and came to a stop at a restaurant overlooking Lake Pontchartrain.

They walked in together, her arm laced through his, into one of the fanciest restaurants she'd ever seen. The smell of seafood, herbs, and spices filled the air and made her stomach rumble. She hadn't eaten all day, she realized and laughed softly at herself.

They were seated, brought a bottle of wine, and menus. Marie looked at the menu, saw there were no prices, and knew what that meant. She frowned, but Matteo had brought her here, so she wouldn't say anything.

They ordered starters and their mains, and then they were left alone. He took her hand and Marie looked at him. There was a band playing soft jazz in a corner, where they could dance, but Marie had never learned to dance.

"I'd ask you to dance, but I have a feeling you don't know how?" he whispered to her as he leaned over the table.

She leaned back a resigned look on her face. "I don't, no. But I could try?"

"That's my girl, always brave." He smiled happily and they went together to the dance floor. He swayed with her softly and told her how to move her feet as they moved around the dance floor. Nothing too in-depth, just a nice, safe dance that became much more enjoyable when she relaxed. She put her head on his chest as the song ended and sighed with happiness.

"You're too good to me, do you know that?" She looked up at him, still a head taller than her, even in the heels. His eyes grinned down at her, just as happy as she was.

He didn't get to say what he wanted to say because his phone rang. He led her back to the table as he spoke into the phone.

"I don't care what Jeffrey wants, we do things my way down here, you get me?" His voice changed, became rougher, a little more menacing. He spoke quietly, so nobody would overhear him, except her perhaps. Marie pretended to gaze out at the lake beyond the wall of glass beside them, but she heard the exchange.

"No, Tommy. You do as I say. Move the shipment, get back to the docks, and stay out of trouble, you hear me?" Matteo waited and must have gotten the answer he wanted. He put the phone away, and then looked at her with an apology on his face. "Sorry, Marie. Business. That should be the last interruption, I hope."

"It's alright. Regina could call me at any

time. We both have lives. Don't worry about it."

She didn't run, she didn't wonder what the shipment was that this Tommy was supposed to be moving. She just wondered what kind of excitement she was in for, the deeper she got into this relationship with Matteo.

20

The date night ended earlier than they expected. They'd had dinner, danced a few more times, and walked through the city for a little while. The shoes began to hurt her feet, so they went back to the car and started on their way home.

"It was a lovely night, Matteo. Thank you." She turned towards him and put her hand on his thigh.

She felt him tense beneath her fingers, but he didn't jerk away, so she left it there. His thigh was like a rock, and she flattened her hand out on it to learn the curves of his leg.

"I'm glad you enjoyed it. You should have nights like that every night." He put his hand down, over hers, and left it there until he had to move it to change gears again. His hand brushed hers up a little higher, and she was the one that tensed.

He'd never let her touch him there, even though she wanted to. He always brushed her hands away or distracted her by moving away. She wondered if he took care of himself a lot because he never got off in front of her. He'd done it over the phone, yes, but not with her there.

"Matteo, can I ask you something?" She waited quietly, her breath held. Was she brave enough to ask?

"Of course, Marie, what is it?" His brows were lowered when he glanced at her, concerned.

"Well, you never... you know. When we're together. You never let me touch you.

You never… get off." She felt like an idiot, but she got it out anyway.

"Of all the things I thought you'd ask, that wasn't it." He chuckled and then took a deep breath. "You're a virgin, Marie. I want you to enjoy what comes before the act of sex for as long as you can before you take that next step."

He stunned her with that. Not because he knew she was a virgin, it was obvious that she was with the things she'd said, but that he wanted her to wait.

"It's not like I was saving myself or anything, Matteo. I just, well, I never had the opportunity to lose it. I'm not sentimental or anything like that, or religious and waiting for a husband. I've just never had a boyfriend."

"Until now," he said and made his claim on her real. He took her hand, kissed her knuckles, and looked at her like she was the only woman on earth that could make him whole. It took her breath away, but he often did that.

"Until now," she repeated. She hadn't been totally for sure until he'd said that. She didn't want to be sentimental, or sappy, and assume that just because he was fascinated with her that he wanted anything lasting. She still didn't know how long he'd be in Louisiana, so maybe she was just a distraction for him while he was there, she'd thought. She wanted there to be a relationship, but she wouldn't push for one.

Her mother had taught her enough about men, by example, and through her words, to know that marriage was a sham and that men always strayed. They'd take what they could get, and then they'd fuck off to the next woman they'd use. But not Matteo. He was different. Everything in her told her that she could trust him, believe him, maybe even… love him.

"You're not married, are you?" she blurted it out without even realizing she was going to ask it.

"What? What brought that on?" He burst out laughing and then looked over at her.

She was serious and her frown showed it. "No, I'm not married. You can search online if you want to. You'll find out I've never been married."

"Oh. Okay." She paused. Then spoke again, relieved. "Good. I probably should have asked that a long time ago."

"Probably," he agreed with a soft laugh. His fingers came out, brushed against her face, and glanced across her lips with a tender caress. "You amaze me all the time, do you know that?"

"Nooooo!" she disagreed immediately. "I'm not special, Matteo, I promise."

"Oh, but you are, lady. Very special." He shifted into a lower gear and slowed the car. They were coming up to his driveway. "You've dug a place into my heart that I didn't even know existed. And you're brave as fuck."

"I'm not brave, just sensible," she continued to disagree with him but was astounded that he'd said that other part. About how she'd dug a place into his heart.

That was big. Very big.

"That may be, but you are brave, lady. I know brave, and it's you, all over." He let his accent deepen, gave her a wink, then turned down the path to his house. "You're pretty damn sexy too."

"I'm glad you think so." Right back to awkward now, she thought. Why couldn't she just take a compliment?

"What do you want to watch tonight? Or do you want to float some more? I actually liked that, I have to say. It was relaxing, and I need that lately."

"Got a lot on your plate?" she asked, just to keep him talking.

"Yeah, we're moving some of our New York operations down here, and, well, it's a whole different world down here, isn't it? Different laws, different ways of doing things. But I'm figuring it out. Nothing to panic over, but it's taking some time to get where I want to be."

"I'm sure you'll manage it. You're a

smart man." She gave him a compliment for a change.

"I'm glad you think so." He gave her own response back to her, with an added wink, and pulled the car to a stop. "So, missy, what do you want to do tonight?"

He leaned closer to her and traced his fingers down her jawline. She grinned up at him, ready for whatever he planned to do. She leaned into him and kissed his jaw. "I'd like to get you naked, and learn every single part of your body."

"Oh, now that sounds nice," he said, but then, they heard an odd noise. When Marie felt her bag begin to vibrate, she knew exactly what it was. She'd set her phone up to ring a certain song when he called. This was just the generic ringtone, and only one other person would be calling her right now.

Regina. Marie scrambled for the phone while Matteo leaned back, concern etched across his face. He knew too.

She did say he was smart.

She fumbled with the phone and then accepted the call with the speaker on. "Hello?"

"Marie, honey, I am so sorry, but, oh, I hate to do this." She paused, and in the silence, Marie could hear the faint sound of her mother's rage-filled screams. "She's bad. Really bad."

"I'll be there in a few minutes." She took a deep breath, looked at Matteo with regret, and then spoke again. "If she gets too bad before I get there, call an ambulance."

"I will, honey. Again, I'm really sorry. I know this was a big night for you."

"I'm sure she does too." Marie knew it was bitter, but she couldn't help it. Her mother was conniving, and if she'd sensed that something was up with Marie, then she'd do whatever it took to ruin it. That wasn't malicious or even petty thinking, it was how Ruby had always been. Her illness hadn't changed her a bit.

"See you in a bit." Regina hung up and Marie sighed. For a second, she leaned back into the comfort of the seat she was in and closed her eyes. "I'm sorry, I have to go."

"She's ill, of course you should go," he said immediately, sympathetic.

"No, she's not ill, she's pissed. She could sense something was going on, and she has to ruin it. She's throwing a tantrum right now. Fuck, why does she do this?" Marie almost screamed she was so upset. Angry even. She didn't want to be angry, but she couldn't help it. Finally, she let out a sound of anguish but sat up. "I'm sorry, I shouldn't have put that burden on you."

"No, I want to help you, Marie, in any way I can. If that's just to vent your frustration, then so be it. You know that's alright don't you, even as a caretaker? You're going to be frustrated, maybe even angry sometimes. It's normal, and you shouldn't feel bad about it."

"Thanks, Matteo." She leaned over, kissed his cheek, and pulled back. "I have to get home before she kills Regina. The longer I don't come to her the worse she'll get."

"That's no way to live." He cringed, but he didn't take it back.

"It's not, but it's been my whole life. I'll text you later, alright? Once I have her calmed down."

"Do that, I'll wait for you." He kissed her this time and got out of the car. "Be careful going home."

"I will," she said with resignation and fatigue. She felt the weight of both as she got into her car, her shoulders drooped. She wanted to lean her head on the steering wheel and cry, but instead, she put the key in the ignition and drove away barefoot, the fancy heels in the seat beside her.

Marie thought about all that could have happened tonight, should have happened, as she drove home. She didn't want to be this angry with her mother, it just didn't feel right, but she couldn't help the way she felt. She was trapped, like an animal in a cage. Only hers was invisible because it was loyalty that bound her to her mother.

It wasn't really love, her mother had never allowed Marie to love her. She wanted to love her mother, sometimes, she even felt it towards the woman that gave her life. Most of the time, however, it was simple loyalty that kept her in the cage she was in.

Nobody else had ever stuck around for Ruby, they'd left, or she'd run them off. In the case of her father, he'd died. But before he died, he'd broken Ruby's heart. She didn't want to prove her mother right when she screamed that everybody left, in the end. That nobody ever stuck around, they all left.

So, she drove home, washed her face off, and scraped the pins out of her hair before she brushed it. She put on her pajamas and took one last deep breath before she went into the room where her mother was still screaming and rolling around in the bed. She watched as her mother threw herself around in the bed, screaming nonsense sounds at the top of her lungs.

"Momma, you either stop this, or I call the ambulance and have them take you to the psych ward," Marie said it quietly, but she knew Ruby heard her. The screaming stopped and the woman's body went still. "You've scared poor Regina to death, and you owe her an apology."

"I don't owe anyone a fucking thing you little slut!" She shouted the last word and turned to face Marie. Her face was red from her exertions, and her white hair was a wild halo that made her look insane rather than angelic.

"You do, Momma. Now, are you going to act right and take your medicine, or do I have to call the ambulance?" Marie waited, her face a stony mask.

"Fuck you. Out running the roads, probably at some dancehall getting felt up by old men for money. Why I didn't..."

"Shut up, Momma!" Marie was the one that shouted this time. She'd had enough.

She couldn't take one more time of her mother wishing she'd aborted the baby that was now the woman that looked after her. "I am not a slut, I'm still a virgin in fact, so put your delusions away. I couldn't get laid in this town if I paid someone to do it, because you, *you* Momma, have made sure nobody wants me. *You* ruined any chance I might have had to do anything in this town. You, Momma, you won't even allow me the time to go on a date because you're so fucking jealous that I might be out having a nice time. Then you have to make it dirty and conjure up bullshit about me sleeping around. It's you, Momma, *you* were the one that was a slut. Not me!"

Regina came down the hall, her eyebrows raised. They were raised in question, but also, respect. She held her fist up and Marie winked back at her.

"Now, things are going to change around here, or you're not going to like the consequences." It was an empty threat, mainly. If Ruby was a danger to others,

Marie would do what must be done, but she knew this was all the dramatic act of a hateful woman. A little brutal truth would calm her right the fuck down. And it did.

"I'm... damn... I'm sorry, Marie." Ruby wouldn't look Marie in the eye as she spoke, but she settled down in the bed. "I'll take my medicine now, please."

"That's what I thought." Marie turned away and walked down the hallway, right to Regina. The other woman took her in her arms and led her down to the kitchen. "That was harsh, Marie, but girl, you made me proud."

"I feel terrible for what I said, but I just couldn't listen to her say she wished she'd aborted me one more time. I just couldn't."

"And you shouldn't, honey. This is hard work, and sometimes it's even harder when it's a relative. Dealing with someone like your mom, well, that's bound to wear on you and you finally stood up for yourself. I'm proud of you."

"I'm glad you are. I'm so out of touch

with normal people, I don't know if I was over the line or what."

"People tend to treat those with disabilities differently. They expect them to be perfect, you know? Does that make sense?" Marie could tell Regina wasn't exactly sure how to say the next part.

"No, what do you mean?"

"I don't know. It's like people think because someone's blind, deaf, or can't walk, that must mean they are innocent of any kind of malice. That they're above the pettiness of those that have their sight, or hearing, or that can move. It's silly, I know, but it's a common thing. And, I might be speaking out of turn, but I have to say it: your momma is no angel, honey. What she was doing tonight? That was just wrong. And what she does to you? It's, well, it's unforgivable sometimes, Marie."

"I know it is, Regina, and no, don't worry, I won't say anything to anybody about what you said. What did she do exactly? Besides scream and try to throw things?"

"She threw herself out of bed somehow. I don't know how she managed it, but she got the rail down and was trying to crawl to your room. I heard her fall out of the bed and caught her before she got too far. Just getting her back in the bed was a trial. I'll be covered in bruises tomorrow."

"I'm sorry. I see your eye is turning colors already." Marie got up, pulled out an empty but clean butter container filled with ice out of the freezer, and wrapped some in a towel. "Put this on it."

"Oh, don't worry about that." Regina protested but she took the ice anyway. "I've had more than one in my life now."

"I was hoping she wouldn't act like that with you. I guess I was wrong."

"I think what you've said tonight will give her something to think about."

"I hope so. I'm trying to hang on, Regina. I'm trying not to put her in a home.

But I can't keep having nights like this. I just can't."

"I know, honey, and you're doing a great job. Don't you worry about that a bit."

"Thanks. Let me get her medicine, and hopefully, we can all get some rest."

It hadn't taken long to get Ruby calmed down this time, thankfully, but it had taken a lot out of Marie anyway. The wall that held back her fighting spirit all these years had finally collapsed completely, and she'd let her own venom out. That's what she was ashamed of. The fact that she'd been mean. But, her mother had responded to it and stopped her hateful ranting. That was a plus, anyway.

21

Ruby's medicines, taken without any more problems, had her asleep within fifteen minutes. Marie suspected the tantrum had worn her out too. Her mother was ill, she knew that, and temper tantrums like she'd thrown, just because Marie was out, would wear her out easily.

Marie slid into bed, texted Matteo, and promptly fell asleep. She didn't even know he'd texted her back until she woke up the next morning. She saw the text, a simple goodnight, and smiled. He'd known how tired she was. How tired she stayed.

She got up, prepared breakfast for Regina and herself, and once Regina left, she fed her mother, bathed her, and changed her gown. Her mother had insisted on pajamas for the longest time, but there'd been too many accidents. Marie got rid of the pajamas and kept her mom in long t-shirts and nightgowns made of thin cotton in the summer. In the winter she had nice fleece gowns that would keep her warm.

Her mother watched her most of the time, silently. Around lunchtime, she finally spoke up. "So, you found a backbone, at last, did you?"

"I suppose I did, Momma." Marie felt a pang of guilt over the things she'd said and stood at the end of her mother's bed. "I'm sorry I was so mean, Momma, but you can't keep throwing temper tantrums just because you don't want me to be happy. I have to get out of here sometimes. If I go out to eat or see a movie, it's none of your concern. At all."

"I see." Ruby pursed her lips, her eyes a

little angry, but she didn't act out. "Good for you."

"Thank you, Momma." Marie had no idea if her mother meant it as a compliment or not, and she didn't particularly care either. "I'm going to wash these sheets and get lunch ready."

"Thank you." Ruby took her eyes off of her daughter then and looked at the television.

Marie was a little shocked, but she didn't let it show. She walked out of the room with her head high and got the chores done. When Jane arrived, she showed her a picture of how she'd looked the night before, a picture Matteo took for her, and Jane acted much the same as Regina had.

"You're gorgeous, girl, and I'm glad to see you got to flaunt it some. How was dinner?" Jane looked tired, but she was still getting over her bout of pneumonia.

"It was nice. Momma threw a major tantrum and I had to come home, but it was a nice night before that."

"I hate to hear you had to come home. You deserved a night out. And that fella of yours sure was determined to let you have a good night." Jane smiled and the tired lines disappeared. "I think you'll have another chance."

"I will. I told her off." She wasn't bragging, just informing the other woman of the night's events. "I really let her have it. She's been much calmer since then."

"It's about time, Marie, I tell you. Good for you."

Marie smiled at the praise and grabbed her bag. "I have to head out to that megastore to get some supplies for Mom, but I'll be back before it's time for you to leave."

"That's fine. I've got time, honey. Just be careful." Jane waved her off and Marie left the house.

She got her shopping done, came home, checked on her mother, and started dinner. In between, she made phone calls about some bills her mother got and wasn't sure the matter was settled when she eventually hung up the phone. There wasn't anything else she could do, for now, so she vacuumed, dusted, and swept the kitchen. Later, she got ready while Regina took care of Ruby. It was a hectic day, and by the time she pulled up at Matteo's she was ready to crawl into bed and sleep it all off.

Matteo met her at the door and hugged her before he led her into the house. "You're tired. Bed?"

"Please. I don't want noise, or food. I don't even want to float. I just want to lie in bed with you."

"That I can do." They went up the stairs to his bedroom and she didn't even bother changing behind the screen. She took her clothes off, slid into the nightgown he handed her from his dresser, and climbed into bed. Her shoes had disappeared at the door, and she slid her feet into the cool sheets with a sigh.

"That is so good," she whispered and let her head sink into the pillow. "This is perfect."

"Good. Want to talk about it?" Matteo had changed and slid into bed with her without disturbing her. The problem was, the moment he slid into bed, she was aware of him.

"I don't, but things keep playing over in my head. I don't have the most maternal mother in the world. She can be... a tyrant might be the nicest way to put it." She felt the pull of his presence and let her hand stray over to his hip.

"I gathered that." His hand came down to hers, covered it, pulled it up. Not on anywhere intimate, but close. Her heart thudded in her chest as anticipation mixed with desire.

"Yes, I suppose you did." She rolled to him, looked into his dark brown eyes to plead with him. "Please, let's not talk. Just make me forget all of that. Please?"

"Whatever you want, Marie." He tipped her chin up to examine her face. "What do you want?"

"I want you to show me how to please you, Matteo. You always make sure I'm taken care of, but you never let me touch you. I want to touch you." She slid her hand over the sheet on his stomach, up to the hard, bare muscles of his chest. His skin was silky smooth, different from hers. But it felt good. "I want to touch you, and kiss you, and make you say my name in that way you do."

"Hmm, let's just keep the sheet between us for now, shall we? Let's start small. Kiss me, Marie." He rolled to his back and she moved over him. Her legs went around his thighs and she leaned over, her elbows on each side of his head.

Slowly, she lowered her head to his and began to kiss him. Gently at first, she pressed her lips to his, before she opened her mouth. His lips matched every movement she made, and she found his tongue the moment she reached out with her own. Desire flared as the kiss became deeper, and his hands came up to hold her waist. Something about his hands there made her want to abandon all control.

His right hand slid up her back, and then back down as her lips lingered on his. She put her weight on one hand and let the other one wander down his cheek. She moved it lower, down his chest, where she found his nipple. Her fingers grazed over it and his hips jerked beneath her.

Ah, a spot he liked, she thought and moved her hand back to flick at the tiny bud. He inhaled sharply, so she decided to try something else. She moved her head down and slid a little lower on his body. Her tongue flicked out to tease at the dark flesh before she took it between her teeth and sucked.

"Oh, now you can't be doing that too many times, baby." He pulled away with a moan. "That will get you in trouble."

"Trouble, huh?" she asked as she wiped her mouth. "What kind of trouble?"

"The kind you aren't getting yet. Behave."

"What if I don't want to?"

"I'll pin you down to the bed and make you scream my name instead." He said it with a raised eyebrow, but there was a spark of mirth there that made his lips twist.

"I see," she said after a second to think. "Fine then."

She loved the images his comment brought to mind, but she really did want to explore him. With a sigh, she moved down a little further. His stomach was flat, hard, and as smooth as his chest. Her hands flattened out on the plain and then moved down his hips. How far would he let her go?

She ran her fingers beneath the sheet and pulled it down. She'd felt how interested he was as her body moved down his. When he didn't move to pull the sheet back, she sat up a little, between his legs, and looked down at him. Thick, hard, and long, the picture had been really him, then. She bit at her bottom lip for a moment as she stared down at him. Unsure of what to do.

With a tentative finger, she stroked the hot flesh, from the tip to the spot where his cock met his body.

She moved over him, fascinated with what he had on display. A hard, muscular body, all hers to use. She leaned on her left arm, over his right leg, and used her right hand to cup the round globes beneath his erection. That made him hiss again and she looked up at him.

His face was impassive, but not angry. She let the globes go and moved up, to wrap her hand around the thick part of him that held her attention now. Her fingers were at least a half-inch off meeting her thumb, maybe more. His hips pulled back as her hand moved before they pushed forward. His skin glided in her hand and she watched as he continued to move in her hand.

"Move your hand, Marie, stroke me baby." His hand moved, but not to brush hers away. He showed her how to touch him, a little tighter, a little faster. She was fascinated with the feel of him. Silky but hard, with the occasional throb that made her eyes widen.

His hand dropped away and she kept moving her hand on him. A glance up showed his head back on the pillow, jaw tight as he tried to control himself. He looked like a god there, with the perfect body, golden tan skin, and those eyes. Eyes that burned when he opened them, burned for her.

"Taste me, Marie. Now." He ground it out between clenched teeth, and that tight feeling she was so familiar with came back. His hips stopped moving and she looked down.

The tip of his cock was slick, it helped her hand to slide along his length. The only light was a soft yellow light from a bedside lamp, and the room was filled with shadows. That drop of moisture gleamed in the low light, and she reached out with her tongue to lick it away. Salty, but not bad.

"Taste it, Marie." The order was harsher,

a sign of just how much his control slipped. He couldn't even modulate his own voice now. That thrilled her so much her nipples throbbed with pleasure as her lips opened to take him inside of her mouth for the very first time. She inhaled his scent, his cologne mixed with something she knew was all him. Her senses were filled with him as he slid into her mouth, the taste of him on her tongue, the sensation of him in her mouth, the smell of his skin, and the touch of his body against hers.

This was what a man tasted like when he was in your mouth, a man that was every inch hers. She looked up to gauge his reaction and saw he was fascinated. He only looked away from her mouth to look into her eyes. Brown eyes met brown and she moaned around him, her body already itchy for his touch. She craved his touch, but she wanted this even more.

"Slow down, Marie." He hissed the words out between his teeth. "Not too fast, it'll be over too quick."

She slowed her movements and sucked harder when he asked her to. He didn't interrupt her too much, she let the sudden jerk of his hip or the way he groaned guide her more than anything. Every movement, every sound drove her to seek more until his hips danced under her in a rhythm she easily kept pace with.

"That's it, Marie, just like that," he whispered, his throat so tight she barely heard him. But she knew she'd found the right pace. She couldn't take all of him, so she used her right hand and her mouth on him. "Fuck, Marie, I can't stop, baby."

She ignored the warning and sucked just a little bit... harder. He immediately responded with a deep, guttural groan which provoked a response in her. She moaned as pleasure shot down her body. Her own hips drove into the bed, but she didn't notice, not when his cock pulsed in her hand and something flooded into her mouth. Not when his cock drove deeper into her mouth and his hands grasped at her hair. He thrust into her mouth over and over again, until he stopped, and something came out of his mouth that sounded like pain, or maybe oblivious capitulation.

She'd pushed him over the edge, and it made her skin prickle with goose-flesh. Amazing.

22

Marie was still thinking about the way he'd just let go for a moment the night before. The sounds he made still echoed in her head, which only distracted her as she tried to clean the house. She'd find herself still vacuuming the living room, going over and over the same spots. Or she lost her train of thought as she cut up vegetables for the gumbo she had on the stove.

She paid attention to her mother, but Ruby seemed to be on a sleeping kick again. Around lunchtime, Marie finally focused and put thoughts of the night before away.

There'd been no actual sex, but it was close. She went in to check on her mother and found she wasn't breathing very well. Jane came in a few minutes later and examined Ruby.

"She's not responding at all. I don't think this is normal, Marie. Where's the thermometer?"

Marie handed Jane the thermometer with a plastic cover to keep it clean and waited.

"Hmm." Jane frowned and looked up at Marie with a frown. "Help me put her on her side."

Marie's pulse jumped and she did as Jane directed. "Does she have a fever?"

"No, her temp's too low actually. And she's struggling to breathe. I want to listen from the back." Jane put the stethoscope on Ruby's back and listened for a long time before she looked at Marie again.

"Call an ambulance. I think she has pneumonia."

Marie's vision narrowed down to the

worry in Jane's eyes and her pulse raced even faster. "Pneumonia?"

"Yep. And no, it's not your fault if she has it. She could have been exposed by me or maybe she has aspiration pneumonia. I don't know, but it's not your fault, Marie. You understand me? I know you, girl, don't blame yourself, you hear me?"

"I won't." Marie looked down at the floor, her brain blank. She wasn't blaming herself, or anyone else for that matter. She was locked on one word that Jane said. Pneumonia. Pneumonia was dangerous for healthy people, for her mother, it could be deadly.

"Call for an ambulance, Marie. We need to get her in a hospital now." Jane nudged Marie back to awareness.

"Of course, sorry." Marie dialed 911 and spoke to the operator.

She walked to the front of the house and waited for the ambulance to appear. It only took a few minutes before the heart-wrenching sound of the siren reached her ears. She heard the sound and had to lean back against the house to stay up. When the crew stopped in front of the house Marie greeted them.

"Hi, are you Marie?" a woman in a dark green uniform asked with a sympathetic smile.

"I am. It's my mother. She's inside." Marie moved through the house, the two female paramedics behind her. She moved out of the way when she reached her mother's room and let them make their assessment.

They ran through the same checks Jane had made, asked them both questions, and then went out for a gurney.

"You made the right call, Marie. She needs to be seen by a doctor," the same woman in the green uniform said and Marie nodded.

"Okay." She looked at her mother, still unconscious, not asleep at all. This could be the last time she was in that bed. But she couldn't fall apart, not now.

"What hospital are you taking her to?" Marie asked, and nodded when the woman told her. "I know it. I'll meet you there."

"Alright. We'll get her there safe and sound," the woman, nameless, but with a face that Marie would never forget, assured her.

"Thanks."

"Marie, do you want me to go with you? I have the afternoon free," Jane asked, and Marie turned to her gratefully.

"That would be great, Jane, thanks."

Jane drove Marie's car to the hospital, and they went in together to find the ambulance had arrived and Ruby was already in a room of her own. Marie went to the room and saw a nurse was already taking blood from her mother's arm.

Ruby's arms were stiff, clasped close to her body rigidly. Her legs were similarly pulled up into her body. An oxygen mask covered the lower half of her face as someone else came in and started an IV line. Marie simply watched and waited.

Someone would speak to her when they knew something.

Jane held Marie's hand tightly, and Marie focused on that comfort that she'd so rarely known until lately. She held onto Jane's hand like it was a raft that kept her from drowning in panic. It felt as though days passed, but Marie had watched the clock. She knew it was only a few hours before the doctor came to find her.

"Which one of you is Marie Hebert?" the woman asked, her face impassive. She was a tall, blond woman with kind brown eyes.

"I am," Marie said from the hard seat she'd taken next to Jane.

"Your mother is going to be with us for a while. I'm admitting her to the hospital. She's got bacterial pneumonia." There were more words, but Marie didn't hear them. She was still stuck on that awful word.

"Marie? Marie?" the doctor called until she saw Marie blink and refocus. "We need you to sign some papers, and then we'll move your mother up to the second floor.

Don't worry, we'll do our very best for her."

Marie nodded, murmured a thank you, but she still wasn't totally in the here and now. She was stuck.

Her mother had to get better. That's all there was to it. A few weeks ago, she reassured herself that the hell her life had been wouldn't last forever. That it would end. She'd been calm about that fact when it occurred to her. Now, faced with the reality of just how quickly that hell might end, she couldn't function.

Ruby was her mother, not a very good one, but she was her mother. There was always a chance that one day her mother might be kind to her, might act like a normal mother, as long as she was alive. If she died, that chance was gone. Marie wanted that chance.

A man brought papers, asked Marie to sign them, and so she did. Jane guided her through the hospital when a team moved Ruby upstairs. She sat out in the waiting area while the new team changed Ruby into a hospital gown and started the lines that would be needed to treat the illness. But deep down, Marie felt it. Her mother had already left. All that was left was a shell.

She could feel it when she walked into the room and looked down at her mother. She took the fragile hand that was so determined to stay at her chest. Her hand was cold, the skin paper-thin and dry. A hoarse sound filled the air, and Marie knew it was her mother struggling to breathe.

A noise pierced the air and Marie turned. "That's my phone, Jane. Can you answer it?"

Marie sat down in a chair at the side of the bed and watched her mother's chest move. She was congested and the sound of her breathing rattled with each movement of her lungs. Would she come back, Marie wondered. Could you come back?

She heard Jane's voice behind her, but it was like listening to sounds from underwater. She could hear the sound, but it was muffled.

The light disappeared, the room grew dark, until a nurse came in and turned a light on to examine Ruby. Marie blinked, looked around, and saw Matteo had taken Jane's place. Her eyes narrowed, her face a mask of confusion.

"What are you doing here?" she asked, her throat almost too dry to speak. She cleared her throat and realized she needed to pee.

"I called you and Jane answered. She's gone home and called Regina to let her know you're here with your Mom. It's almost midnight, Marie, let me take you home. There's nothing you can do here, tonight. You need to rest."

Marie turned away, looked at her mother, and closed her eyes. She felt a tremor run down her wrist and into her hand. She'd held the same position for hours. Her mother hadn't come back, not yet. She probably wouldn't.

"Okay," Marie whispered. "You can take me home."

"Good," he said and came to help her stand up.

She hadn't realized her legs had fallen asleep until she stood up. She leaned into Matteo, and a sob broke through the numb wall that had blocked all thought. He held her as she cried, made sounds to soothe her, and let her cling to him with a tight grasp.

"Come on, baby. Let's go home. They'll call if something happens."

Marie nodded and wiped her face. He picked up her bag, took her hand, and helped her out of the hospital. He drove to a fast food place, grabbed some food, and she ate something, but she had no idea what. The wall went back up after her tears dried.

When he had her in bed, wrapped safely in his arms, her head against his chest, she asked him for one thing.

"Peace, Matteo. Please give me peace."

"How do I do that, Marie?" he asked and

brushed a lock of hair from her face. "What do you want me to do?"

"I want you to," she paused, swallowed, and then looked right into his eyes. "I want you, Matteo."

"You don't want to wait, Marie? Until a time when you're a little more certain about it? I don't want you to regret anything." He kissed the tip of her nose, and that made her giggle.

"I've felt like I'm dead inside all day long, Matteo. My brain is just off. I want you to make me feel alive again. Yeah, I guess we could wait until a more romantic time, when you've had time to plan out every-thing just right. But I don't want to."

"Hmm. Well, let me just do two things, first okay?" He grinned a teasing grin and got out of bed. She laughed because she knew he always had to make things just right, even when she wanted spontaneity.

He went to his dresser, pulled out two brand new candles, cinnamon apple from the scent she smelled, and then put on music. It was something she'd never heard before, sultry, with pulses of deep base, but no singing. Whatever it was, it was sensual, and she liked it. She liked it even more when Matteo moved in time with the music, his eyes on hers as he made his way back to the bed.

She sat up on the edge of the bed when he curled his fingers at her. He came to her, took her slim wrists, and placed them on his shoulders. He was in his usual attire of pajama pants only, while she had on a new nightgown he'd bought her. A navy-blue satin and lace slinky little nightgown that she'd loved, but had been too numb to truly appreciate. As she looked up at him now and saw the way his eyes moved down to the lace triangles that covered her breasts, she knew he'd made the perfect choice.

Everything else in the room disappeared as he went down to his knees between her legs. "You're beautiful, Marie, and far too good for me."

"I'm yours, Matteo, whether I'm too

good for you or not." Her fingers traced over his lips, down his neck, before she looked into his eyes.

"Those innocent eyes of yours drive me crazy, do you know that, Marie? They taunt me when you're thinking dirty thoughts, they beg me to fuck you in such a sweet way that I can barely stand it. Lie back, baby. Let me taste you." He pressed his hand on her shoulder until she did as he asked. "Put your feet up on the bed, open yourself for me."

Again, she moved as he instructed, ready to do whatever he asked of her.

"More, Marie. Open, baby." He nudged her feet further apart, and she let her knees go. That's when he moved, slid his tongue between her folds, a slick hot touch that brought every single nerve in her body to attention. Her hips rocked up, to meet that surreal sensation, to ask for more.

Her fingers clenched on the bedcover, a thick red coverlet, but she didn't care what it looked like. All she cared about was Matteo's tongue on her, the way his lips closed around her clit, and *sucked*. Her skin went tight all along her body and she shivered as he pushed the satiny gown up over her hips. He wanted her nipples, but the material wouldn't go up that high.

He guided her hands up instead. She slid her fingers into the lace and found the buds hard and tight. She knew how to do it now, he'd shown her. Stroke the tips with the tip of her finger, he'd told her, and she'd learned that she could make herself pant, even if it wasn't quite the same as when he did it.

His hands, now free, slid under her ass to tilt her directly into his face. Long, swift strokes teased her into a breathless moan before he sucked at her clit again. One hand slid out from under her ass to tease at her folds, at the entrance that had never been invaded before. That made her shiver all over again and she breathed his name on a sigh.

His face was smooth against the tender

skin of her inner thighs, his hair a silky tickle that only enhanced what he did. She was open to his stare, his to command, but all he wanted to do was please her.

Sensations swirled: pleasure, desire, curiosity, need all raged through her as his tongue worked over her. Everything whirled inside of her, and when she squeezed her nipples just a little tighter, the spark, that thing she was so eager to reach for, turned into a flame that burned through her. She lost everything then, even herself, as he sucked, and sucked, until it all exploded outward.

"Matteo..." she whispered just as pleasure shot directly into her brain, a new drug she couldn't live without anymore. Never again would she be able to go without this wondrous substance that only Matteo could give to her.

She heard him between her thighs, a thick groan, his own heavy breathing, and wondered if he was more eager than ever, more ready than he had been before because he knew this time, he'd have all of her? That only made her go even higher, that stray thought.

Matteo moved suddenly, wrapped her legs around his waist, centered himself at her opening, and then thrust into her with one quick jerk of his hips. It wasn't sweet and soft, it was savage, eager, and the only thing she wanted right now. She didn't want soft and sweet, she wanted raw and real, and that's what he gave her.

There was pain, but she'd always been an active girl, even without sports, so there wasn't much to force his way through. It ended swiftly, the pain, and became a foreign sensation. A full sensation that she couldn't compare to anything else.

She heard his heavy breathing go quiet as he inhaled deep and long. He'd stopped the second he was inside of her. He let her adjust, until her hand fluttered down to his, where he held her hips. He moved her legs, pulled them up over her shoulder, and moved impossibly deeper inside of her.

"Fuck you're so tight. Take a breath, Marie, relax, and I might just get all of my cock in you." He sounded calm, but his fingers were tight on her and she felt a shiver go through him. A slight groan from him, she breathed, and then, he moved again.

He wrapped his fingers around her wrists and held them tightly as he began to move. She couldn't move, she was *his*, and she loved it. She gave herself up to every thrust he made, every withdrawal, as he moved into her, out of her, and right back in. She felt something, something good deep inside and arched her hips a little, until he hit that spot and something brand new started.

"Matteo, there, right there." She heard him grunt and then he pushed in again, in hard, tight strokes that made her throw her head back in total surrender.

She moved with him in the end, though she didn't realize it. Her ass pushed up to meet his hips every single time, as her inner walls pulsed around him, as the world exploded all over again. Only this time, that empty feeling she hadn't known was there, was filled, and she made a new sound.

A sound of pure satisfaction that also sounded self-satisfied, because she was. That was oh so perfect, and she never wanted it to end.

Her nails scratched at his hands around her wrists as she came apart beneath him. That sensation of pain must have driven him over the edge because she felt him pulse within her, that same pulse she'd felt when he came in her mouth, and she gasped all over again, flew apart all over as he joined her in the bliss-filled world they'd created together.

23

The next morning Marie woke up sore, tired, and not ready to face the day. She was ready to face Matteo, though, and grinned when he brought breakfast to her.

"I know you like pancakes, so I brought you these, with sausage and maple syrup. There's coffee and orange juice, or apple juice if you prefer."

"Thank you," she said and pulled her head back when he leaned down to kiss her. She put an extra kiss on his cheek as he pulled away to put the tray over her lap.

"Today, I'm yours all day long, Marie. I

know you'll want to be at the hospital, so I've cleared my schedule. I've also made it clear that your mother is to get whatever care she needs, whether her insurance will cover it or not."

He didn't expect thanks, she knew that, but she said it anyway.

"She's your mother, Marie. You love her. I couldn't do anything for my mother, but maybe I can for yours."

Marie doubted anything would help her mother now. She'd felt it yesterday, her mother was done. Ruby had been trapped in that bed for years now, she had no real life anymore, not like the one she'd lived. She'd given up, now that Marie could stand up on her own two feet. She was ready to go. Not even Marie's pleas or Matteo's money would keep her here anymore.

"She's done, I think, Matteo. She's had a hard life, and she's tired. I don't think anyone or anything can save her now."

"I understand that. I'll be there for you,

though, no matter what. I want you to know that."

"I'm glad."

She ate her breakfast, they showered, dressed, and left for the hospital. A pang of guilt lanced through her when she saw her mother's lifeless body on the bed. Instead of staying here with her mother last night, she'd been making love with Matteo. There was nothing she could do about it now but stay right here with her mother, until she either woke up or passed on.

She thought she loved Matteo, she felt it in her bones, so she let the guilt wash away. She'd needed the comfort he gave her, and it had been beautiful, beyond words. She'd wanted that feeling to last forever, and it mixed with the grief she felt now. Later, she could have his love, for now, she needed to focus on Ruby. He knew that. That's why he'd brought her here, and told her he'd stay with her.

She sat at her mother's bedside, took her still-rigid hand, and breathed deeply. Ruby's breathing wasn't so labored, but it was barely there now. Her skin had a gray pallor to it that was enhanced by a dryness that lotion couldn't fix. This was her body trying to protect itself. All the energy, liquid, vital nutrients that she got were going directly to her organs and nowhere else.

Marie might not have had much of an education, but she read a lot. She knew about her mother's condition, what would happen as her body began to shut down. She knew the science of it all, but that didn't help the grief she felt.

"Marie, you're here. Good. I wanted to talk to you." The doctor that Marie remembered from the day before came in. Today, her blond hair was scraped away from her face in a ponytail of curly hair. Dr. Amanda Johnson, her name tag read.

"Hello, Dr. Johnson," Marie said and stood up. "What did you need to talk about?"

"I've had her GP come in and we've talked about your mother's case. She has a 'do not resuscitate' order in place, and you have power of attorney, so it's up to me to talk to you about what's going to happen."

The doctor took a seat next to Marie and Marie pulled her bottom lip in. She knew what was coming, what the doctor would say. That didn't make it easier to hear.

"Your mother is not going to recover. She had a stroke before the pneumonia set in. She's only going to get worse and her orders won't allow us to put her on life-support. She may last the day, but I don't know if she'll last much longer."

"Thank you," Marie said woodenly. There it was. The truth. Her mother was about to die.

"Do you want to know more, or should I give you some time?" the doctor asked with a sympathetic tone.

"No. That's about it, I think. I just have to wait now, don't I?" Marie's eyes filled with tears and she brushed them away.

"Thank you, doctor, really. I'm just trying to process this."

"No problem, Marie. I want you to know, I'm here if you need someone to talk to. From what Jane told me, you have spent a very long time caring for your mother. I know this must be very hard for you now."

"Thank you," Marie repeated. She hated the words now, she said them way too much, but there was nothing else she could say. "I appreciate that."

"The nurses will page me if anything happens."

"Thank you, doctor," Matteo said, and came to take the woman's place as she got up to leave. She left the room and Matteo took Marie's hand.

"Are you alright?"

"No, but I'll have to be. She's... dying. I have to be alright, until the end, anyway."

"I'm here, Marie."

"I'm really, really, glad you are." She leaned over to lay her head on his shoulder.

Jane came in at lunchtime, and Matteo

went down to the cafeteria to get them food.

"Hi, darling," Jane said as she wrapped Marie in a hug once Matteo was gone.

"Hi," Marie whispered back and hugged Jane tightly. She pushed the tears away and pulled back. "Thanks for coming, you didn't have to."

"The agency hasn't filled this time slot yet, so I thought I'd come by and check on her. They told us she wouldn't be going home."

"No, it doesn't seem so." Weight, grief, sank down over her in a dark cloud, as she realized that the next time she went home would be the first time she was there without her mother in years. That her mother would never be there again.

Emotions warred inside of her as she sat there with Jane. The relief of freedom at hand made her feel even more guilty than having sex had. Grief that she'd never get that chance to measure up in her mother's eyes. Or maybe she had.

"You know that day you told her off, Marie?" Jane piped up suddenly, her voice sure. "I think that was the day she knew you could go on without her. She wasn't the world's greatest mother, but she knew you were ready to face what was on the way."

"Do you think so?" Marie asked. "You don't think I caused the stroke?"

"Not at all, honey. She was bed-ridden and she had pneumonia. You didn't cause that stroke at all, Marie."

"I hope not." It was a thought that had been playing in the back of her mind. Now it was out in the open, she remembered the last words her mother said to her. Her mother told her thank you. Maybe she had gotten that last chance to measure up, after all, she just hadn't noticed.

"Thank you, Jane. That's put my mind at ease," Marie spoke again.

That was the moment machines started to beep, loud noises that alarmed Marie immensely.

Jane pulled her away as nurses rushed

in, followed by Doctor Johnson. They looked at Marie, and Doctor Johnson held her hand out to Marie. "Say goodbye, Marie."

"What?" It had happened so quickly, way too quickly. "She's not gone yet. Can't you just do CPR and get her heart to work again?"

"No, honey, they can't. She has a DNR, you remember?" Jane whispered.

"But... she was alive just a minute ago. This isn't right. She's..." Marie looked down at her mother's face. It was slack now, peaceful, far more peaceful than she'd ever seen it before. "Gone."

"Come on, Marie. Let's let them do what they need to do." Jane pulled her from the room, and Marie followed stiffly.

She was even more numb than she'd been the day before. Her mother was dead. She knew it was real, but it couldn't be. She was alive only a few minutes ago, and now she was gone. She slipped away without a sound, gone before Marie could say anything. But what would she have said?

Marie's world tunneled down to her own breath, her own heartbeat, as people brought papers for her to sign, as Matteo asked questions she couldn't answer but tried to. A nurse came and asked what funeral home she wanted them to call, and Marie didn't know. Jane provided that answer. There was only one in their town, so it was obvious, but Marie couldn't think.

She made it into the car with Matteo, and she managed to get through the ride home. It was when she walked into the house that she finally collapsed. He was right there behind her, kneeling over her to protect her from anything, anyone, as the sobs finally tore free from her soul.

"She's gone," she kept repeating. In whispers and screams, the words came out. Her mother would never again be in this house. She would never call out for Marie, or eat the food Marie made her. She'd never ever see her mother's eyes, or feel her touch. It was all done, gone, because her mother was gone.

And in the back of her mind, in some secret place that was swathed in guilt, was another word that she didn't want to think about it, but it repeated, it clashed with the other words that she could speak. Free. She was free, at last, and it felt so wrong to think it. But she couldn't help it. After all these years, she was free. So why did it feel so wrong? She clung to Matteo, curled herself into his body, and cried out the pain, the grief, the misery that had plagued her for so very, very long.

24

Marie looked around at the empty ceme-tery, a public cemetery because her mother had been ex-communicated from the Catholic church. She was alone except for the officiant. She didn't know who the man was, didn't know his name, though he'd said it.

She closed her eyes as his words droned on, hidden beneath the umbrella as the rain poured down over them both. The grave must surely be filling with water, she thought, as she stared down at the empty hole. Beside it was her mother's casket. A plain thing, it lacked any sort of ornamentation and the only flowers on it came from Jane, Regina, and Matteo. Marie added a sprig of roses from the bush in the backyard, and that was the final token of respect from anyone that Ruby received.

Marie had put an obituary in the local paper and the Times-Picayune, so that if there was anyone out there, some long-forgotten relative that might want to attend the funeral they would know the time and place. Marie stood alone, though, and somehow that seemed to be how it should be.

Jane had been given a new patient to care for, as had Regina, and their lives would go on. Marie's was paused, however, stuck in that same moment of grief. The sloshing sound of tires on a wet road intruded into her mind and Marie looked around. Matteo stepped out of the car, a black raincoat over his black suit, and walked to her.

Without a word, he put his arm around

her, took over the umbrella, and stood with her as the unknown man droned on. Marie watched the man, in his late 40s, paunchy, with a balding head of black hair. His glasses kept getting splattered by rain, but he didn't stop to dry them. He held a paper in front of his body in one hand, with an umbrella in his other hand, but he never deviated, and Marie suspected he knew the mournful words by heart.

The words finally came to an end, the man spoke a few last words of respect to Marie, and he left. Marie turned to Matteo, her eyes wide, the skin beneath them bruised with grief.

"What now? Do I just leave her? Do they leave her here and put her in the ground later, when it's stopped raining? Or do I wait for someone else to come and do it now?" She had no experience with funerals. She didn't have much experience with anything, come to think of it.

"They'll do it, darling. Listen," he paused, stroked her face with gentle fingers, his eyes full of something that she could only call mournful. Maybe something akin to regret? What was going on? He answered before she could ask. "I need to talk to you when you're ready. I have to go out of town tonight, and I'm sorry about it, but I have to go. When I get back, there are things we need to talk about. About your mother. Her past, and well, we can discuss it later. I have to go, I have to pack, but I'll be back soon, alright?"

"What? What do we have to talk about, Matteo? Can't you stay, just tonight?" She didn't want to admit it, but she didn't want to walk into that house alone today.

She'd gathered her things up that day he'd brought her home, and then she'd run out of the house, once she'd finally been able to stand up. She'd been at his house the last three days. Now, she'd have to go back to her house alone?

"I can't stay, baby. I'm needed in New York. I would stay if I could, I swear it, but I can't."

"Alright. I understand." She blinked rain out of her eyes, or maybe it was tears. She didn't know anymore. "Be careful. And call me."

He left and she turned back to the grave. The flowers had fallen from the casket as the rain pelted down. They'd slid down into the grave and Marie's eyes began to sting. This was how it ended then. This was her final moment with her mother.

"I'm sorry it was only Matteo and me, Momma. I guess you probably knew it would be, though. You lived your life trying to push people away. You couldn't push me out, though, no matter how hard you tried. I did good by you, I was a good daughter, even if you never said it. I hope you've found peace, at last, Momma. Goodbye."

She turned away just as the rain started to fall down even harder. The drive back to the house was strange for Marie. It was so familiar, the route, but the world had suddenly become a different place for her. She was alone.

She had Matteo when he got back from New York, but otherwise, there was no one to worry over her, nobody to care about what happened to her. That feeling only got worse when she walked into the house. The machines in her mother's room were quiet now, turned off by someone. Probably Jane, or the paramedics that took her mother away. She didn't know.

She stood there, in the doorway at the back of the house, and looked into the kitchen. She wanted to shut the door, speed over to Matteo's house and beg him to let her stay there while he was gone. She knew she had to do this at some point, though. She knew she had to face the truth.

She kicked off her plain, black flats, and made her way through the kitchen. For years now, the kitchen had been her domain. Most of the house had, but she hadn't changed anything. She'd left it as her mother wanted it, in case there was a miracle cure that came along and fixed her. In case her mother might be able to get up and walk into the kitchen again.

Every surface was clean and tidy. Everything had a place, and all was in order. She hated it, right now.

She moved into the hallway, thought about going into the living room to watch TV, but that room down the hall called to her. If she closed her eyes she could hear the oxygen machine that helped her mother breathe. She could hear her mother call to her, could smell her still, even though she was gone.

Marie walked into the room, turned on the light, and wondered what it would be like to sleep in this house now. Her eyes spotted the air conditioner, and she decided that if she had to stay here, for once, she was going to sleep comfortably.

She knew it was all distraction, that she should probably wait and have someone else do it, but she couldn't. She took the AC out of the window in her mother's room, lugged it down to her own room, and fiddled with it to get it snug in her bedroom window. When the unit came on and started to fill her small room with cool air, Marie sighed. She smiled and laughed at her own silliness.

Her back ached, but she didn't care. She had air conditioning in her room, for the first time ever. She had peace and quiet, and the certainty that she wouldn't be woken up in the middle of the night to clean up another human being. For the first time, she let herself think it, without guilt.

She was free. She could do whatever she wanted, go wherever she wanted, be whoever she wanted to be. Thoughts began to spin wildly around in her head. So, instead of doing anything, she curled up on her bed and rested.

She must have fallen asleep because it was dark when she woke up. She checked the phone Matteo gave her and saw he hadn't messaged or called. Odd, but something was going on there.

He'd said something about her mother's

past. What could that possibly mean? She didn't know but wondered for a moment. Could he be some relative of her father's? He was from New York, but would he sleep with her, knowing they were related? No, that was insane. They weren't related.

He probably just wanted her to talk about the years of abuse he suspected she'd endured. That was more than likely it, she decided and got up to go find something to eat. She saw the mail she'd collected from the mailbox and wasn't surprised when she saw a bill from the hospital.

They hadn't even given her time to grieve. She set it aside and went through the rest. Condolence cards from the businesses her mother had been associated with over the years. The pharmacy, the local grocery store, so small it knew when one of its customers passed away, the doctor's office. Even the agencies that had sent Jane and Regina sent cards.

She put them all in a pile, and that made her brain click. What would happen to the equipment in the bedroom? Her mother had paid for it all. There wouldn't be anyone coming to collect it. She'd have to sell them somehow, she decided.

Which made her think about her mother's clothes. Her jewelry. It was all fake, except that diamond ring she'd held onto for dear life. Marie went back to her mother's room, dug the jewelry box out of the dresser, and brought it back to the kitchen.

Trashy costume jewelry filled the box, but a few pieces weren't too bad. Marie put aside some earrings, a couple of cheap but pretty rings, a silver bracelet, and two that must have been gold. Marie had no idea how to tell if any of it was real, but the two gold bracelets hadn't faded so they must be real. She put them all aside and decided to ask Matteo about the rest of the jewelry before she put it in a yard sale.

She'd decided that's what she would do. She would put everything up for sale, see how much she could get, and what was left, she'd give to charity. She'd keep the furniture and appliances she used until she could replace them, and then she'd get rid of that too. Maybe she'd even paint the rooms, cover up the awful colors that decorated the walls now.

That's how she'd fill the empty hours until she found a job. She decided she'd give herself a few days, and then she'd call the agency that paid her. They must need someone with her experience? And she was used to the work now, they wouldn't even have to train her. She knew what to do.

Marie wasn't exactly happy, but she felt a little better. She had a direction to go in now, a plan, kind of. She took out a bowl of gumbo from the freezer and put it in the microwave. She wasn't hungry, and she couldn't taste her food, but she knew she had to eat.

One day, this grief would leave her, and she'd have to go out into the world. The world had no idea she existed, and she didn't know a whole lot about the world out there, but she'd have to find a way to settle into it, one way or another. Her phone rang, and she answered it without really looking to see who it was.

"Hello?" she said, happy that someone had called her.

"Hi, Marie, it's Jane. How are you, honey?"

"Oh, Jane! Hi! I'm alright. Glad you called." She really was glad. She'd started to feel lonely, there in the house alone.

"I'm sorry I missed the funeral. I couldn't get anyone to switch shifts with me."

"It's alright, Jane, really. It was dreary anyway. Well, I guess most funerals are, but the rain made it terrible." She fiddled with the pile of cards as she spoke. She knew she was only speaking to fill the silence but couldn't help herself.

"Are you alright there by yourself? I could come over later if you want company."

"That would be nice, actually. Matteo

has to go to New York for the next few days, and well, I'm all alone."

"I know you are, honey. I'll bring pizza and some videos. We'll have a girl's night in, shall we?"

"That sounds great, Jane. I look forward to it." Marie pushed the bowl of gumbo away and sat up a little straighter. "Do you have a DVD player by any chance? I only have a VCR, and I don't think anybody has tapes for those anymore."

"Actually, I have an embarrassingly large collection of movies for VCRs. I'll bring some of my favorites, and I'll introduce you to some classics."

"That would be great, Jane. Thanks."

"No problem, it'll be my pleasure."

Marie hung up the phone and got up to clean the bowl she'd used. Jane didn't have a family, her husband died in a car accident when they were both 33 and she had never remarried. Her husband hadn't been able to father children, but Jane didn't mind. She liked taking care of her patients and she'd devoted her life to doing just that.

Now, she was going to be Marie's friend, a real friend, and come stay with her for a little while. That meant the world to a woman that felt entirely alone. Marie knew she had Matteo to lean on, but he'd be gone, and she really needed someone to keep her company at least.

Jane was that someone and Marie thought that it figured it would be Jane. The woman was as kind as she could be.

When Jane arrived, Marie let her in, and they went into the living room. Jane had several bags in her hands, and she handed one to Marie. "These are the tapes I brought. See what tickles your fancy and we'll get started. I've brought chips and dip, microwave popcorn, and some sweets if we decide we want that at some point."

"Jane, you didn't have to do all that." Marie looked up at her friend and smiled. "But I'm glad you did. It sounds great!"

"Well, I could stay at home with my cat

and watch Netflix, or come over here and keep you company. Sylvester will wait, he hates me anyway. Silly cat." Jane sat down on the couch, spread out the goodies she brought, and pulled out a bottle of wine and another one of apple juice. She knew Marie preferred that in the evenings to soda, and that made Marie smile again.

It helped when people noticed things about you. She pulled out a movie from the pile in the bag and held it up. "What's this about?"

The cover was kind of scary looking and the title was "12 Monkeys".

"Oh, that's a good one. And it has Brad Pitt in it, you'll probably like it, judging from the books you read."

"Alright. Let me just get everything turned on, then we'll be ready to go."

Marie had been certain she'd spend the night miserable and alone, yet, here she was, sliding a VCR tape into an ancient VCR, so they could watch a movie on the ancient TV. It wasn't so bad after all.

25

It was the quiet hours of the night that got to Marie. Jane helped to fill the quiet hours of the evening, but it was the night that spooked her. She hadn't slept in the house on her own since she was a child. Not since her mother got ill and stopped carousing, anyway.

Marie tried not to think about the past too much, but since her mother's death, memories haunted her. Things she didn't want to remember popped up in her head all the time, and she was on the verge of seeking out a psychiatrist. The problem was, she had no money.

There'd been a nest egg when Marie was born, but Ruby had gone through that. The last of it went to pre-pay for Ruby's funeral. Now, there was nothing left and bills were starting to pile up. She had to pay the power bill, the water bill, and the cable bill with the $300 she had left in her own bank account and try to pay off some of the other bills with what was left in her mom's account. There wouldn't be anything left after she did that. The Social Security Administration wouldn't pay benefits to people that were dead, after all.

Matteo had said he'd pay for the medical costs, but what about the rest? She had to renew her insurance on the car, the insurance on the house, and she didn't have a job to pay those bills with. She'd started to get strange bills in the mail, debts that were owed from years ago, and she didn't know where they were coming from.

She wanted to talk to Matteo, but he'd been strange since the funeral. Even when he did call her, his conversations were stilted, not like him at all. She was worried he'd gone back to New York and found a woman that was more suited to his tastes than she was. Yeah, he'd said she was the most beautiful woman in the world, and insisted she was too good for him but was that really what he thought?

Men were pigs, according to her mother. If the men she'd drug home with her, back in her carousing days, were anything to go by, Ruby had been right. Married men, single men, drunks, bankers, fishermen, tourists, she'd had them all, and that could only mean she knew a thing or two about men, right?

Her books said differently: that not all men were the same, but that hadn't been what real-life showed her at an early age. Hell, a few had even tried their luck with Marie a time or two. Her mother had always caught on quick, though, and got rid of the bastards before they could really hurt Marie. She'd always glared at her daughter, told her to stop being such a little whore and the men would leave her alone. Marie didn't know what she'd done to be called a little whore, so she couldn't stop it, so she just avoided all contact with any man her mom brought home.

Was that who Matteo was? Was he one of those jerks that would take advantage of any woman he came across? Would he tell her all the things women wanted to hear, only to move on to the next one before he'd even washed off the smell of that last one? She didn't think so.

He wasn't that kind, her instincts told her that. He was a good man, in his own way. She suspected the rumors about him being in the Mafia were true. He was involved in some kind of organized crime, he had to be. She'd overheard a conversation or two about shipments, and how the law was breathing down their necks. She'd ignored them, acted like she hadn't heard, but she had.

The idea fascinated her. He was part of some kind of criminal underworld. He had power. A power that she didn't have. She wanted some of that power, and one day, she'd ask him how to get it. For now, she'd just wait and see what he wanted to talk to her about when he got back.

He'd said it was about her mother.

What could he possibly have to say about her mother?

A few days ago, she'd pondered whether he was related to her. Maybe he was part of a different Mafia family than her father? Or maybe he was some kind of lieutenant? Sent down to take care of her father's little girl?

She let that one play-out for a while. She'd never known her father, and her mother called him a pig, the same as the other men. Marie knew the truth, that her father had been married to someone else, but slept with her mother anyway. Maybe her father had set up a will for any children he might have fathered, and Matteo had come down to give that to her?

She'd be a millionaire and would never have to worry about anything ever again, in the fantasy. She'd never have to work, or struggle, or buy the cheap brands of products she wanted. She could go on vacations!

She'd go to Italy first, then France. Maybe to England. Or Iceland! She'd have tons of money she could go where she liked! But it was all a fantasy, and she had no money to speak of. Her father's family had never cared about her, and his wife certainly wouldn't have. According to her mother, the wife got it all anyway. There'd been nothing Ruby could do.

Marie wondered if her mother had ever really tried though. She hadn't found anything in her mother's papers that would have shown where she'd filed suit against Marie's father's estate or asked for child support payments from the estate. She wasn't sure if that was a thing, but surely there must have been some way that Ruby could claim some of that money? The man had been rolling in money.

Marie hated all these thoughts about money and felt dirty for even thinking about it all. She was just lost at the moment and had no idea what to do. Jane had been a help though. She'd told Marie that she could probably get on with the agency Jane worked for if the one Marie was paid by didn't want to keep her.

"They're always looking for good people and you have the qualifications, so don't panic too much. Not yet, anyway." Jane had told her after their last movie night.

Marie decided to do something else besides sitting at the table and worrying. She sent Matteo a text, but he didn't answer, so she went out to mow the grass. The weather had started to change, and the dark came earlier now. The kids were already back in school, so fall was on the way and then winter.

Down in her neck of the woods, it didn't

get extremely cold, but it felt like it did to her. She'd have to get all of her winter clothes out soon and give them a wash. She wondered if it was the last time she'd mow the grass that year, as she put the mower away a few hours later. She cleaned off wet grass from the bottom and put it in the storage shed.

When she went back into the house, she checked her phone. Still no message. Something was definitely wrong. He always responded within 15 minutes of a text from her.

They'd had sex, was that it? He'd got what he wanted, then her mother died, so now he was off like a shot to get away from the grieving woman? That pissed her off a little bit. He could have waited until she'd recovered a little bit, couldn't he?

"Or is this his way of letting me down gently? Stilted conversations and no text messages?"

Another thought crept in, one she hated, but still, it dug into her brain. Maybe he's married and can't really talk to her when he's with his wife? He'd told her once to Google him, so she picked up her phone and opened the web browser. She put in his name and found quite a few people who matched.

The first one was the one that mattered though. His picture was there, and it had some information about him. His birthday, his single marital status, and the fact that he had no children. He apparently worked for his family, but there was no real information about them, just links that linked to new pages full of useless information. Shipping was the one thing she could understand. They were involved in shipping.

That could be anything though. Cars, goods from around the world, anything really. It could even be that they shipped goods out of America, not into it, she thought. The good news was, Google said he wasn't married.

So, what was his problem then? Was he in meetings when she called? New York was an hour ahead of Louisiana, but she tried to be aware of that. And he didn't say he was busy, he just didn't... talk like he normally did.

His responses were all staccato, yes and no, with no questions, only responses. She didn't like it, but she couldn't really say that, because he never gave her time. It would end with, "listen, I gotta go", then he'd hang up.

His emotional distance hurt her so much she didn't even want to call him now. She had enough pain to deal with. She put the phone down and decided it was time for that yard sale.

She'd started to clear out her mother's room and had made headway with the clothes. That was all on hangers and up on a moveable rack. She'd kept some of her mother's vintage dresses, heels, and a few other things. She'd started to feel less bleak without her mother there, and her normal logical brain had started to kick in.

She pushed the rack out to the living

room and started to box up other things. All the drugs went into the toilet, and down the drain. Marie decided she could use some of the lotions and creams her mother had, and the pillows she put into space-saving bags and sealed up. She put those in her own closet. She didn't want to think about it right now, but the pillows still smelled like her mother, and one day, she might want that back.

All the extra sheets and towels that Marie knew she'd never use went into another box, as did a few of the knickknacks her mother hadn't broken. Marie didn't want them, they only reminded her of the ones that *had* been broken. She didn't want that, so she put them in the yard sale box.

Then Marie thought about some of the pictures on the walls. People Marie didn't know and didn't care about. The frames might get a dollar or two, so she put them in a box, and before she knew it, she'd taken down pictures, got rid of other knick-knacks, put away decorative glass her mother had collected, and had even put in a few of the plants she'd watered religiously but hated.

The house felt emptier, with each box she stacked in the living room, but it kept her busy, so she didn't want to stop. She ignored the sound of empty echoes and kept going. It didn't matter how many rooms seemed bigger now, without all that junk her mother had put in them. If she was busy, she didn't think about Matteo coming home and telling her they were finished. Or wonder about his cryptic last words to her at her mother's funeral. She was too busy dusting off empty shelves and dismantling bedframes to think, and that was just fine with her.

Once it was dark, and she was too tired to move, she took a shower. She stood in the bathroom, alone, with all the doors locked. She'd locked the front and back door, and the door to the bathroom, but she still felt spooked as she looked at the fogged-up mirror over the sink. It was a tiny room, but she'd used it her whole life.

For a moment, panic overtook her, and she stared at the door. She couldn't go out there, what if someone had quietly broken in? Everybody in town knew she was alone now, even if they didn't acknowledge that her mother had died. Or that she even existed. What if there was some crazy out there that wanted to get to her?

"Stop being so paranoid, Marie, there's nobody out there." Just saying the words out loud made her feel stupid. She rolled her eyes at herself and opened the door. She didn't want to admit it, but she felt relief when there wasn't a crazy killer on the other side.

She went to her mother's room and picked up one final thing to keep for herself - the television. All she could get were the free-to-air channels, but she'd watch repeats of 'Frasier' all night if that's what it took to get to sleep. She'd also kept some of her mother's sleeping pills. Just in case. She had a feeling she'd need it, so she made herself a cup of hot chocolate, went back to her room, changed into her pajamas, and put the television on.

She looked at the pill for a while before she took it. She didn't want to get addicted to them, but it wouldn't hurt for one night, would it? She took the pill quickly, swallowed it down with her hot chocolate, and then settled down in the bed. The TV was on, some program she didn't know played loud enough to drown out other noises that the AC didn't hide. Her bedroom door was locked, and she stared at the ceiling.

She could do this. If Matteo left her, she could learn to live on her own. Eventually, she'd stop being so afraid, too. She hoped. Her heart would break into a thousand tiny pieces, and she'd probably die from it, but if she lived, she could totally do living on her own. She knew she could. As long as he didn't tell her he was her cousin or some weird stuff like that first. Then she might die of shame.

What was that part about wanting to talk to her about her mom's past? It nagged at her until she fell asleep, just as clueless as the day of her mother's funeral. He'd be home in a couple of days. Then she'd find out. Whether she wanted to or not.

MAFIA'S FAKE BRIDE

I hope you enjoyed reading Mafia's Dirty Secret. If you're anxious to find out what's going to happen between Marie and Matteo, here's a little sneak peek… Enjoy!

Summer xoxo

1

Matteo learned a lot in the two days since he'd arrived in Louisiana. The first thing he learned was a young woman was living with the target. Ruby Hebert, according to the report he'd found online, had lived at the same address with the same girl since she'd left New York.

He'd paid for the report from an online data-broker. It turned out the girl, now a woman, was Ruby's daughter, Marie. There'd been a school picture for the young woman, and an old picture from the DMV for Ruby. The young girl was cute, in the way young girls were, but she was of no interest to Matteo. Too young and not part of the job. His target was Ruby.

Further digging showed that Ruby was now an invalid and taken care of by her daughter. Which meant he'd have to take an interest in the daughter. This bit of news changed things and he'd had to email Celeste about it.

She'd come up with a new plan, a plan that involved him wooing the daughter. Whether she was attached to someone or not. The way she saw it, some backwater bumpkin from the sticks would be happy to leave any kids and a husband behind for a man like Matteo. Then, he'd dump her, with her life in shambles and with her mother's debt to pay, due on demand.

He'd almost run away at that point when he'd read the email. Most people would say fine, you can't get blood out of a turnip, but not Celeste. She wanted Ruby to pay, and if that meant using the daughter to do it, then so be it. If it got him that one step closer to his goal, he'd do it.

He wouldn't like himself, but Matteo knew he hadn't liked himself very much since Celeste took over his upbringing. She'd turned a bright, intelligent, happy young boy into a somber, watchful robot that barely felt... anything. His father had disappeared a long time ago before he was even born, but his mother was still alive.

Matteo couldn't even respond emotionally to her, which was why he hadn't seen her in months now; maybe it had even been a year, he wasn't sure and didn't care. Emotions were not something he allowed himself to feel. Especially when Celeste was near him. He just shut down completely when he was near her.

Being this far away felt good, really good, but he knew she was there, in the back of his mind. She would be waiting, judging, ready to use anything, and anyone, for her brutal version of revenge. Not that she didn't deserve some kind of revenge, her husband had been a cheater, and then he'd died because of his activities. With his lover, not his wife.

Nick, Celeste's now dead husband, had branched out their organization, had started to creep into territory that wasn't his, and it cost him his life. Of course, those activities had allowed Celeste the life she loved, but Matteo wouldn't point that out. He inhaled slowly, deeply, and then walked away from the laptop.

The sound of a bell told him he had a new notification and he walked back over to the laptop. He didn't want to look at the new email, but it might be important. A click of the mouse opened up a new screen and he saw a picture of a very timid looking young woman. It was her driver's license photo and she stared straight into the camera, no smile, no emotion at all. Just a dead gaze that still managed to stir... *something* in him.

A frown marred his features as he increased the size of the photo. So, this was

Marie now. Well, from her latest license, at least. He stared at the image for a moment before he closed the picture and read the text within the email. It seemed Marie's mother no longer drove, but Marie did drive her mother's car out every day, around one in the afternoon, to do the shopping and other errands.

He wrote back to the data broker to tell them it was good work and then glanced at the clock. It was about the time the young woman drove into town, so he picked up the keys to the old car that his aunt had provided.

The 1966 Lamborghini 400 GT was the very same one his uncle had died in. Celeste paid to have the damned thing restored for some reason, and now he was expected to drive it around town. Matteo assumed it was to creep Marie's mother out, to frighten her, but the woman never left her bed, so the whole thing was pointless. It drove smoothly and had a few updates to make it suitable in the modern world, so he didn't mind too much.

With a cold gaze hidden behind mirrored aviator sunglasses, he drove into the small town, careful to keep his speed down. He wasn't in a rush because he was waiting to spot the girl. He figured she'd stop off at the grocery store first. With a twist of his wrist, the car turned smoothly into a gas station where he filled up the almost full tank. He glanced around and saw her, over in the parking lot across the street.

He didn't know for sure, but he was almost certain she was staring right at him. He felt his lips twitch in satisfaction, his target had been located. He put a debit card into the machine, paid for his fuel, and then slowly drove across the road and into the parking lot of the grocery store.

Matteo noted she was distracted as she put the groceries away. She turned to return the empty cart to the stand, then stopped, obviously lost in thought. He drove on but slammed on the brakes suddenly so that it made a noise. He felt a prickle of guilt, not enough to make him feel sorry, but he felt it.

She responded with a turn, fear clear on her face as she stumbled a little. Her hands were on the hood as he stepped out of the car, all that was good and humble as he apologized to her.

He wasn't aware of what he said, or what she said. All he could do was note how white and perfect her teeth were, how beautiful and haunting her eyes were, and just how long those tanned legs of hers were in those tiny denim shorts she had on. The t-shirt tented over full breasts that drew his gaze for only a heartbeat, it was those eyes that fascinated him.

His thoughts flew right out of his head for a moment as he looked at her and took in just how odd he felt when he saw her up close. The pictures had done her no justice at all because she had a lovely, heart-shaped face, clear tanned skin, and the cutest button of a nose.

Matteo wasn't completely dead inside, he still liked to have a woman when the mood struck. Usually, they were women that knew the score and were in it for what they could get out of him. This woman was all innocence and charm. There was no kind of guile in her eyes, no knowing twist to her full, luscious lips. And all of that black hair of hers made his hands itch in ways to touch her that he'd never felt before.

He came back to reality briefly, gave her his card, and apologized once more. The target had been acquired and the first contact had been made. That was all he needed to do for now. He left her to carry on with her errands and went into the store to buy a few things, so nobody would notice that he'd gone into the parking lot but not gone into the store.

His aunt wanted him to be noticed so he went over to the library briefly, picked out a book, and got himself a library card. He left there and drove on, thoughts of the girl, the woman rather, still on his mind. He turned on a playlist he kept hidden in his phone and hit play. The sound of The Beatles filled the car as he drove back to the mansion hidden down a bayou path.

It wasn't until he was in the driveway, the voice of John Lennon in his head, that he realized he felt something he hadn't felt in a long time. Desire tinged with something he thought might be hope. That made him blink a few times before he turned the car off and stepped out.

Now, why would a girl from the back of beyond in Louisiana make him *feel* anything? Was that what had happened to his late Uncle Nick? He'd met a woman that he couldn't take his eyes off of, or had she just been another conquest? Matteo was familiar with conquests, women he'd bedded for prestige, women he'd bedded that had refused him, but he'd charmed them over time. They'd given in to him, just for him to dump them after their conquest.

Would this woman be the same? Would

he be able to seduce her, as his aunt wanted him to do, and then leave her with a broken heart and a debt she couldn't possibly repay? He'd had another notification about their finances: they were one unexpected bill away from the poorhouse, so he knew the women wouldn't be able to repay his aunt. Would the girl's broken heart be enough for her?

Somehow, Matteo doubted it. The whole situation was far thornier than he'd expected it would be. But then, he'd expected a woman like any other, easily conquered and discarded. Something about this young woman told him that wasn't going to be the case.

He thought he'd be able to keep his heart out of it, he had little doubt about that, but would he be able to forget her? That was a question he didn't want to examine too closely, so he went out to the pool instead. A few laps would keep him focused, and when he went to rest an hour later, his mind was clear.

He had a mission; he would do his duty.

He owed his allegiance to Celeste and the family. Make that family with a capital F. That's who would protect him, serve him, make him their king. This girl meant nothing to him, and he'd do what was expected of him.

She stayed on his mind throughout the night, however, and when he went to bed, it was her he dreamed of. Long, slow kisses made him hum with pleasure, even in his sleep, as he stroked the full breasts, he'd barely noted earlier that day. She wrapped herself around him, eager to know his touch.

At that moment, in that place, Matteo finally felt free of the mental restraints that had shackled his thoughts for so long and he surged against Marie's body with his own. He was just as eager as she was, he craved the devotion those dark brown eyes of hers promised him, craved the solace of her embrace. Even more than that, he accepted it all from her, he expected it, demanded it as the moments passed and he felt her soft body melt into his.

Every inch of her was cradled against him and he slipped the shoulder of the white gown off of her shoulders, to kiss the smooth skin there. He inhaled deeply, about to lose control, but he restrained himself, just for now, just until she begged him for more, for all of him.

The gown slipped lower, to the very tops of her breasts, and Matteo shuddered as he let his lips skim the plump flesh. She felt so good, so right. Nothing, no one, had ever felt so right in his entire life, and he felt the pulse of that sensation deep inside his abdomen as a twist of pleasure. It was a pleasure that radiated out, to the very part of him that he wanted to bury inside of her.

"Marie, you're mine. You'll always be mine," he murmured against the tops of her breasts as he felt her shuddering response against his own body. It only made him hungrier for her.

His hands moved from her waist to her

back, to lift her against the wall so that he could cradle himself between her heated thighs. It was so warm there, so promisingly wet, that he could feel her against his suddenly naked body. He didn't know how his clothes disappeared or why, and didn't care, he just wanted to move, to pull back far enough to bury himself inside what he instinctively knew was her virgin sheath.

He'd pulled back, teeth set, ready to hold back as she took him inside of her body for the very first time. A piercing sound infiltrated the moment, destroyed it, as reality invaded. He was dreaming, that noise was his phone. Fuck.

He rolled over to answer the ring and saw it was Celeste. He couldn't quite shut down as he normally did when he had to speak to her, but he faked it well.

"Yes, Aunty?" he asked in a bland voice, no sign of his anger at her or tiredness to be found in his voice at all.

"Did you meet the girl yet, Matteo?" Celeste came straight to the point, without even the courtesy of saying hello.

"I have, Aunty. She's going to be… pliable, I believe," he reported, despite the inner voice in his head telling him to hang up and get back to fucking the sweet temptation that had filled his dream. Would he be able to recapture that moment now?

"Good. You need to do this carefully, Matteo. By that I mean, don't invite her to dinner tomorrow and fuck her tomorrow night." Celeste had always been able to cut to the heart of the matter, and when the moment called for crudity, she could use it. Even if it was her nephew she spoke to. "I want her well and truly in love with you by the time you have your way with her. Then, you're going to crush her, do you understand me, Matteo? No gentle letting down, no sweet parting, I want her crushed."

"Yes, Aunty," he said without a hint of emotion.

"Good. And Matteo? Don't fall in love with the little guttersnipe, do you hear me?

It wouldn't do at all." Celeste was just as cruel to him as she was to anyone else. He heard the sound of her nails tapping against the wood of her desk and cringed. He hated her, but she was the head of the family.

He would do as instructed.

I hope you like what you've read so far. Mafia's Fake Bride is now available on Amazon
www.amazon.com/dp/B08KFPFBWL

An Amazon Top 100
A 5-book billionaire romance box set
Filthy Rich
Summer's other box sets include:
Too Much To Love
Down Right Dirty

Mafia's Obsession
A hot mafia romance series
Mafia's Dirty Secret
Mafia's Fake Bride
Mafia's Final Play

Screaming Demons
An MC romance series full of suspense
Take Over
Rough Start
Rough Ride
Rough Choice
New Era
Rough Patch
Rough Return
Rough Road
New Territory

Rough Trip
Rough Night
Rough Love

Check out Summer's entire collection at
www.summercooper.com/books

Happy reading,
Summer Cooper
xoxo

ABOUT SUMMER COOPER

Thank you so much for reading. Without you, it wouldn't be possible for me to be a full-time author. I hope you enjoy reading my books as much as I do writing them.

Besides (obviously!) reading and writing, I also love cuddling my dogs, shouting at Alexa, being upside down (aka Yoga) and driving my family cray-cray!

Follow me on
Facebook | Instagram
Goodreads | Bookbub | Amazon

Get in touch at
hello@summercooper.com

www.summercooper.com

Made in the USA
Coppell, TX
19 August 2021

60821758R00249